HELLO!
MY NAME IS
TUNES

by

Francis Voignier

Cover design by Francis Voignier
Artwork: iStock license

This book is a work of fiction whose characters bear no resemblance with real individuals. All coincidences are hence deemed purely accidental.

Library of Congress Cataloging-in-Publication Data
Voignier, Francis 1954—United States
Hello! My Name is Tunes/Francis Voignier
ISBN-13: 978-1-952858-02-4
ISBN-10: 1-952858-02-X

Metaphysics – Philosophy – Cats

francisvoignier.com
Dolosse & Writs, Eureka, CA

CHAPTERS

01 – How it Ends—*Page 1*

02 – The Beginning—*6*

03 – The Landlady—*13*

04 – Close Encounters—*15*

05 – The Winds that Spoke—*20*

06 – The Long Journey—*24*

07 – Perspective—*30*

08 – Early Phase Two—*36*

09 – Later Phase Two—*44*

10 – The Deeper Reality—*50*

11 – Second Move—*62*

12 – Phase Three—*69*

13 – Initiation—*80*

14 – Perspectives—*88*

15 – Assignment—*92*

16 – The Paradox of Fear—*102*

17 – Clarity—*110*

18 – My Name is Tunes—*117*

FROM THE AUTHOR

Tunes was a remarkable being—a magical one. The past tense does little justice to how much his life still affects my very present and how far, I am sure, it will resonate, until the time comes for us to meet on new grounds.

To say that he lived a full life is nothing short of an understatement—he lived it with unbound joy backed by rare wisdom.

He stole my heart from day one and kept it close to his for sixteen years. I knew from that moment on that my life would never be the same.

He was my dearest companion, always close-by during extremely difficult times, and the greatest teacher I ever had. To say I miss him is a misuse of the term—I adored him—and at times it seemed that my existence revolved around his. In truth, we had found each other at a unique trailhead, one that led to an extraordinary and still unraveling journey.

5th October, 2020

My deepest thanks go to my life partner,
Reverend Elisabeth Zenker,
for her love and unending support.

1 – HOW IT ENDS

Of all the names my Papa gave me, my favorite is Tunes. Of course, he's not my father, but he might as well have been.

I knew there was danger where he so often advised me not to go, but I love exploring so much that I couldn't help it! It wasn't the best of deaths; I got out of body pretty quickly though. Let me be clear, the dog is not to blame—he acted as he was trained.

I love my Papa to bits. I know he adores me too—now, as strongly as ever—even though I am free from the physical. When I was just a kitten, looking at him straight in the eyes, I fell in love right then—we were in it together for the long run. And what a run it has been! Sixteen years in cat time is a mighty long life—I am forever grateful for having shared it with him and Mama Lisa. Ah, and the three of us meeting and bonding the year of my birth—what delicious synchronicity!

I wanted my Papa to find my dead body—my love forbade letting him worry sick for days. When I saw him pick me up and kiss me behind the ears, my soul melted like my beating heart did every time he did so. I was a bloody mess, but he didn't care—at that moment, we were as close as we could ever be.

—o—

I sit between the two of them, Mama Lisa facing my Papa. She, summoning spirits from across the thin line that separates the physical from the spiritual—a true medium; he, my Papa, quite deft at it too, but in a different way; more like a human whose faith runs so deep that his belief in the afterlife stands unflappable. He's right, for there is such a place—actually, many places.

From my position between them, I am filled with the joy of knowing they accept the timing of my exit. I can't say it didn't take me by surprise, but I was aware of it being around the corner. My concern was about the way of getting out of body, something I didn't excel at naturally, but I'm proud of how it happened—it was definitely quick, as I said.

Although, I could have gotten used (maybe) of living the life of a domesticated cat, especially with such abundance of love in the house, I very much doubt it would have served what I had in mind when I chose to return to the physical as yet another feline. Exploring is my thing and I love the outdoors. I even fancied getting soaked in the rain—*Aqua-kitty* being another name that popped up on occasions.

But let's face it, even though I was particularly fit for my age, and quite healthy from eating the best of foods served with so much unconditional kindness, I sensed the first physical hiccup a few days before parting, in the form of one of my front legs seizing. It didn't escape my Papa; I could read his thoughts and he knew I did. Just saying we both understood what it meant. I had no intention to drag the three of us, for the short rest of my physical existence, into a spiral of decay; that's no way to return the love. Plus, my Papa had already done so much for me when I had erred on the wrong side of caution at roughly the same time last year; although I wasn't quite ready to leave then.

As the result, I lost quite a bit of my freedom, but I took it as the natural extension of that mistake, in the hopes of earning it back—which I did.

— o —

When Mama Lisa calls me from across that thin veil, I'm already there. I mean, how can I not be? Even though I am so happy with my new place and the prospect of boundless adventures, I don't see the point of not staying connected with a life I cherished and experienced to the fullest. The three of us made the choice of spending a feline's lifespan together for the specific purpose of enrichment of the soul—all of it part of the greater *now*, indelibly forever. What I learned and discovered through this incredible journey with these two exceptional humans is what allows me to be here helping my Papa's pen find its words. When I say I am one with him, I mean it with unrestricted conviction.

As I recall the details of my last minutes on Earth to my loved ones, so flows the eternity of that time spent together, and the many encounters with the wild that brought me so close to my demise on so many occasions. To come face to face with creatures of the forest, regardless of the dangers, filled me with incommensurable joy. To be chased by fox, deer, and bear alike was some of the greatest thrills of living up in the mountains, by the river where I was born. I call it phase one. There were three of them—pretty impressive by cat standards!

But before I go on recounting those magical years, it is best I explore what makes my connection with my Papa, and to some big extent, Mama Lisa, so special. The latitude I was given to exist both in close connection with humans, while free to explore my potential as a feline, has few comparatives in my sphere; it's either one or the other, give or take various degrees of measured mixes around food, as well as shelter during adversary conditions. We chose each other for the very purpose of traveling on a path rarely taken, that of recognizing our place in existence with the full understanding of our separateness as species and our undividable bond as spirits—why my Papa also called me *Professor Tunes*. I can't begin to tell you what joy the thought brings me.

— o —

My Papa could always read my mind, unlike other humans that came to the houses. Of course, I could read his most of the time—it was like water running from the ground, clear and hypnotic all in one. His voice was a long drone that soothed me when he whispered behind my ears, but it was also thunderous and sometimes scary on the rare occasions of our disagreements; but those were almost like encountering the wild—invariably grounding me when I lost my sense of direction. Apart for those few isolated incidents, the entirety of our life together was filled with love, gentleness, and mutual admiration for what we deemed to be the magic of this union; the three of us, for that matter, magical beings on our way to a glorious and mysterious unknown.

I cannot count the ways my Papa demonstrated his affection to me. It was selfless, unconditional. He cleaned my litter box as if it were a ritual of the highest order, always anticipating my joy of finding a clean place to relieve myself when the weather was too harsh for me to explore. Instead, the exploration was in the details of our relationship, in the way he made sure I was treated like a guest of honor, with clean bowls for the gift of delicious food, especially when he added a touch of hot water to it. How delighted I was to watch him do so! And the grooming, oh my, the grooming, daily, fine-combing my hair, between my ears, the side of my face, down my neck and my front legs, and along my sides where it tickled, until I bit the comb for him to stop. He did, for he knew when too much was too much, but it was never too much behind the ears—it always made my tongue stick out with pleasure.

— o —

All of this brings me to reflect on my life in such vivid colors and crisp sensory impulse memories, that my Papa is awakening to its potency. I sense that he too is seeing his life being replayed in better focus. Mama Lisa does such a great job at carrying my voice across the veil, but let it be told that from my standpoint, cat or not, languages are all one and the same, so, English it is!

I could say that by not heeding my Papa's warnings about the dangers of leaving the beautiful blooms of our magical garden, I paid a heavy price, while taking the joy right out of his heart. But I am assured it isn't so—he knows the timing is right, and through the tears, he is rejoiced of knowing that I am in a very happy place. I promise we will meet in the dream state, for I tell him how much I love dreams. He can't wait, he says.

——— o ———

2 – THE BEGINNING

I shall start with a picture my Papa keeps close to his heart. At the time, there was nothing to it; I acted spontaneously, fully in tune with my environment, but now I see why the deed was so special to him. He and I were sitting at the edge of the front porch, looking towards the gardens. To our right, at the base of one of the deer-fenced apricot trees, Bobo—the landlady's cat— and my sister, Fenderina, were making circles, deeply intent on catching the mouse inside the wire mesh guard. It went on and on, and finally, I got bored. I leaped across the lawn, climbed the cage, got inside, caught the mouse, climbed back out, and brought the fare back to the porch as a present to my Papa. But insisting that I had earned it, he offered that I should eat it; which I did with much enjoyment. In the meantime, the other two cats were still making circles around the cage, oblivious to what had just happened! This makes me realize how close the two of us, Papa and I, already were, for, to my knowledge, no cat alone would have done what I did.

— o —

I have fond memories of our long walks to the rivers, the big one by the flat, and its tributary, accessed through a wooded path onto a sand bar. Oh, the bliss of those times, the incredible, accelerated sense of being, all the newness of a world full of scents that spoke of native flora and messages sent from creatures lurking in the shadows—so much danger for a kitty, yet so much excitement! I climbed big rocks and trees, rested in the coolness of ferns on the hot afternoons of summer, my Papa always close by, watching my back. Oh, the incommensurable joy of exploration!

There were times on the flat when I felt it was best to skirt the open, as birds of prey circled the great skies. Eagles, ospreys, hawks... each and all on the lookout for an unsuspecting soul the size of a meal. It was a game best played with all senses tuned in!

On one of those walks, I ran ahead of Papa and Mama Lisa, around a curve at the end of the property where the woods thickened, to come face to face with a bear—a grumpy one—who took offense at being caught off-guard. He came running after me with great speed, back around the curve, only to find me at my Papa's feet. "What are you going to do now, Mister Bear?!" He quickly stopped in his tracks, reluctantly turning around and grunting his disapproval of my manœuver.

In perspective, I think it was a very funny moment. I had so much trust in my human protector, for that was how I saw him, this *big* Papa of mine. It is why the bonding can never be undone.

— o —

There were many walks to the rivers, especially during the hot days of summer and fall. We, my sister and I, would run to exhaustion, panting with our tongues hanging out. At first, the Bobo came too, but soon got tired of it, and before long, Fenderina stopped joining as well. She had other plans, plans that eventually got her in the same kind of trouble that saw my demise, but hers was eons ago, for by the time of my death, I had long forgotten about her. I don't think we ever bonded, unlike me and the Bobo for a while—he was kind to me, taking me under his wing to teach me what he thought I should know. He was supposed to hate all cats, but he liked me and Fenderina, and I am grateful for it. He didn't die a good death, I gathered, from reading the pain in the landlady's heart and thoughts. We all loved the Bobo.

—o—

Since my assignment was about the human connection, I learned a thing or two about people's way of thinking. So, before it comes to it, now is the time to debunk an old assumption. "Do cats go to cat Heaven?" No, there is no such thing as cat Heaven—or Hell for that matter—nothing but fields of potential where all kinds of kindred spirits interact in the most joyful of ways. We're all parts of a larger script, cats, humans... Offstage, it's a whole different situation, though one may say that the three of us share a life away from the physical limelight. But I have told too much already—it's not easy to convey these thoughts at my present stage.

—o—

There were many cats that came and went at the river place. Wild and skittish Calico seemed to have been there forever. She fully disliked me and viscerally hated the Bobo, but one day, this fellow, Neon, arrived—a low-to-the-ground, fluffy orange kitty—and it was love at first sight! Calico had never been so playful—I was happy for her, even though I wished she had never been around. But soon Neon was gone, with just the length of his chewed up spine left in the lawn as a reminder that he truly was there. Calico never recovered from the loss—before long, she too was taken.

And then there was Mocha, a big ball of a cat, who had the nerve of hissing at me in my house on arrival. She scared me at first, since I was still impressionable, but soon, I was the one who hissed at her. She simply didn't belong, but she was Mama Lisa's handed-over cat from her daughter; why my Papa couldn't say no. I saw him try to ease the deep pain with which she came. It helped a bit, but it didn't prevent her from dying of those wounds—she was born with them, but couldn't find the way to let go of them. In the end, I stopped hissing at her.

But the one thing I remember most about Mocha is the one day she walked in the lawn in front of the house, when this bobcat came out of nowhere to attack her from her blind side. She was so fat that he failed at wrapping his teeth around her neck, allowing her to twist around and scratch him with all the repressed fury bottled up in her body. For a moment, they were like tumbleweed that had gone mad, but soon she was back on the deck, while, he, the bobcat, scuttled away, all bloodied up and limping. It was very impressive; and boy, was I proud of her! Sadly, she didn't seem to care.

There was Beatty, the Bobo's sister, deaf, blind, and febrile. She slept all the time as if she had missed the date of her passing, resigned to wait till her body ran out of its own will to live.

Then came Brazen, the king of adventure, who went farthest than all and made a point of marking our property as the last post of his travels—a mighty achievement considering he lived on the other side of the wide and uncrossable river. He enjoyed his life to the fullest, inspiring me to hone my skills as an explorer, although I had a different view on how to go about it.

It's also possible that Brazen was before my time and that I am mixing my Papa's memories with my own, but it makes no difference in our case, which I hope will become clear as to why, as we go.

— o —

But while many rewarding adventures happened during daytime, night was when most of the action took place. Aside from the landlady's flashlight, on and off scanning the darkness at unpredictable hours, nocturnal reality belonged to the wild, and to some extent, the semi-feral, such as us backcountry cats.

Although bears were by far most ubiquitous in lieu of their stature and sheer abundance, they posed little danger to us kitties. My kind of action was to observe from a safe place, for I understood too clearly that the open was nothing but trouble. Calico and Bobo knew it too, but their hatred for each other often took them into chases across the moonlit fields. Mind you, the raucous would turn the predators into observers of their own. Papa would get up to break them apart, sometimes up high in a tree at the farthest end of the property.

The danger was truly in hunters, mostly bobcats, lynxes, mountain lions, coyotes, and the occasional desperate fox, but one could never underestimate the ferociousness of raccoons and fishers amidst accidental encounters.

The mountain lions would come in rhythm with the moon cycles, a reflection of the size of their overlapping hunting grounds. I don't recall seeing more than one at a time out of a total of three or four, hence the overlapping. They were incredibly stealthy, but not enough for my Papa, who could sense their presence, like the day he tried to keep Fenderina inside the house to no avail. She must have known it was her time, considering how intent she was to not heed the warning. Needless to say, she never returned.

— o —

In spite of much vigilance on my part, there where instances when I couldn't help introducing myself to strangers. It wasn't necessarily an instinct of mine, knowing that the deer are herbivores, to guess that a close encounter with a doe rearing her kids posed an issue. Actually, as I learned, cats of my size were seen as cubs better killed before they grew into dangerous predators. But for reasons best ascribed to my blissed ignorance, nothing happened when I came nose to nose with that mother deer surrounded by her three newborn. Well, she did twitch, which let me know it wasn't the smartest thing to do, but I got a serious thrill out of it—part of the exploratory items so dear to me.

So, I went on meeting extraordinary characters; chasing some, while being pursued by others, in an exhilarating game made so by its edge of danger. My Papa was oblivious to these meetings since he slept at night, but I'm rather sure he would have disapproved of some of my methods. For me, as opposed to other cats I met in my long life, danger was always part of what made life rich in focus, and for that, a certain distance had to be kept from humans as to not depend on their rules.

I was blessed with a Papa who understood that I had to do my things, while he kept an eye on me whenever he could, never oppressive in his watch, always naturally loving. It made me even freer to know he was there, taking great pleasure in observing my explorations. From where I stand now, I realize that he was learning from me. It doesn't get any better!

—— o ——

3 – THE LANDLADY

The landlady went by a name, but I'm not at liberty to mention it for reasons best kept alone.

She loved cats, was good to them; although there was something that made me hesitate as to how far I wanted to go with the affections. Perhaps, she was a bit too sure of herself as a cat lover, failing at comprehending that there is far more than cuteness, fur, and oh so precious habits and personalities to us—or at least, that's how I saw it in my regard.

Fenderina must have perceived in her something I didn't, for when Papa and Mama Lisa had to absent themselves for matters of the highest order; she deserted me to join her, leaving me to sit the house, while I patiently waited for the return of my loving providers. Of course, the landlady was very kind, feeding me and spending time with me, but she also resented that she had to do it, which is why I stayed put.

It was my understanding that Papa loved the landlady. They had been friends for years ahead of my arrival, but I could have told him that his love was wasted on her, for she didn't possess the qualities necessary to reciprocate. She was the center of her own world, which we all are, but with her, it came with an emotional vortex. Interestingly enough, my Papa's attraction to her was not unlike my own to danger, but in his case, death would have taken a whole different meaning hadn't Mama Lisa joined us at the most auspicious of times, which as it turned out, was the year I was born. Nonetheless, it was the landlady who insisted that my Papa adopt an orange kitty as part of moving to the property. Why orange? Well, some say we're the best, even though it's up for debate, but I agree that color in cats is a crucial element to personality. So, why did she also insist that he adopt my sister, who was all black with a patch of white on her chin? Humans are complicated.

In all fairness, the landlady was the catalyst to making my relationship with my loving and dearly loved providers possible. There is purpose in every act, which doesn't mean awareness is necessarily part of the process.

———— o ————

4 – CLOSE ENCOUNTERS

There are all kinds of dogs, and as a family, they are rather unpredictable. Unlike cats, who more or less share a resemblance from one group to the next, dogs can look utterly alien from one another. Nothing new there, but what's remarkable about them is that as much as their physical appearances differ greatly, nothing could be as disparate as their characters. They are sponges ready to absorb the qualities of their owners with an uncanny sense of duty and extraordinary dedication. You learn more about their masters through them than those masters will ever allow you to know about themselves. That's why I cannot put the dog that killed me to shame.

That being said, there are those who viscerally wish to bring all cats to their deaths, most notoriously Boxers, who, because of it, become subjected to some of the most spectacular dares by semi-feral tabbies.

One such dog, a redoubtable female, belonged to one of the landlady's friends. I barely escaped her on her first visit to the property, and believe me; when I say I was not at all prepared for it is an understatement. That dog attacked me when I had my back turned—luckily my Papa was around to avert disaster!

Then there's the dog that acts all playful at first, but incrementally becomes aroused to the notion that game can be more fun with ample saliva, and inevitably, blood thrown in. There are no limits to the frenetic kind.

In my life, I have made a point of not trusting any of them, including those whose owners claim they're good with cats. But I will make an exception for the one who was my Papa's best friend before me, even though I have never met the dog in question. I believed him because a loving heart never lies. Of course, the miniature ones are no issue, aside from the hysterics. Needless to say, it's somewhat ironic that my general mistrust in them proved me right in the end.

— o —

I find it interesting, in a poetic justice sort of way, that I should be dictating these notes through the spiritual channels that connect me to my Papa, when, in the first place, I made sure he would never know about the details of my nocturnal escapades. I am assured that he is beyond passing judgment, as I should have known from the beginning. He only sought to protect me from harm, and not to prevent me from doing what was necessary to my evolution—why he always said, "Be safe, my boy!" How much I love him for his keen understanding and generosity of heart!

— o —

So, what happened during those nights, and what is the thrill I speak of?

The thrill is anything that arouses the senses in a way that justifies the physical experience, when the hormones take body and mind to an unprecedented level of elation. Every bristle and nerve end gets activated to the point where danger and safety wed into a vital union. It is the apex of experience, the point at which past and future coalesce into an everlasting present. It is the essence of private reality, the distillate of all that is in a single drop of pure energy to be used to further the unique travels of the self.

For me, coming within proximity of the unknown of others, their uniqueness, their signature scent, the spirit within their flesh, was the thrill in question—and it still is. When I speak of exploration, I do not mean journeys across vast distances, but rather of odysseys within the infinity that lies beyond communing with these souls.

Although I am mostly covering encounters here, the same goes with everything that lives and wishes to share, may they be flowers or trees. Needless to say, not everything needs to involve danger to be exhilarating. Take songbirds for example, specifically the pair that followed me everywhere for months before I departed; there was no threat as to them coming within reach—I was the threat—yet, they couldn't help coming a bit closer every day. I let them do it, for I understood too well what it meant at their private levels. One may say that they went through the motions of protecting their young, but I know better—no species is that disconnected from their reality, at the exception of humans perhaps. I'm of course not referring to my Papa or Mama Lisa, whose sense of the wild is very much alive within them.

— o —

The thrill, I must say, doesn't exclude natural safeguards integral to one's projected lifespan. Mine kept me blessedly protected. Predators knew it as well as I did, which afforded me closer proximity and a better sense of depth as to their beings. In a way, spiritual connectivity overrode instincts, for they too benefited immensely from these meetings. Above all, timing was essential, since the drive to hunt couldn't be put on hold forever—I had to know when to disengage before it was too late, hence the safeguards. One could say that their universe is safe until the last of those protections is used. When my Papa whispered into my ear his last, "Be safe, my boy!" I knew that my time had come. How did I know it was his last? It carried with it a simple, shared code we both wrote and understood; something that came with our contract way back when I looked in his eyes for the first time, and saw much love ahead. He wasn't surprised when I died—just overwhelmed with loving emotions.

—o—

So yes, for the first half of my life, I came to meet and know many residents of the wild, respectful agents and perpetuators of the natural order as it exists from root to star. Since it was my principal assignment to get to understand what lived within the ego-personalities that provided us, felines, with love and food, souls that could just as easily torture and mutilate to quench impossible thirsts, I witnessed how disconnected humans were from the hand that nurtured them. As they protected themselves from the things they feared, just as equally, they repressed the skills that connected them with the vitality of their origin as a race. Without that modicum of danger, those whose unique visions enriched my life, while allowing me to successfully complete my studies, would have been absent. Paradoxically, without my Papa, and to some great extent, Mama Lisa, nothing would have been the same. Rather, other life scenarios would have come knocking at the door—none of them as suitable as this one. The multiplicity of choice is of the essence here, and

I must add that the greater the awareness, the sounder the picking—courage and trust, love and joy, work and play—all the attributes that bring purpose and the wish to excel into clear focus.

— o —

Effectively, and in feline fashion, I am moving sideways, evading the dramatic side of those encounters. But not really, since drama is only one of the ways to accent experience, for there was never any of it during my most dangerous moments. The intensification of the senses, the pumped adrenaline, the pounding heart... were all part of following the flow of knowledge from its effervescent beginning to its resting place. Just like life, each was a minute version of the greater multidirectional sequence.

——— o ———

5 – THE WINDS THAT SPOKE

There were moments between Papa and the landlady that felt like doom had descended. Those were so intense that I could feel the entire property, as a gestalt, come to a pause. Their voices would echo through the valley, charged with such rage that they might as well have been mythical figures fighting to the death. There was much power tapped from dark places, and frankly, it scared me.

That was when I knew a fundamental fissure had ripped the land of their relationship open. It was a battle of will between two souls that conceded no grounds. It was the beginning of a steady descent into coldness and resentment. On one such day, the wind spoke of change; a new turn that would take me away from a place I loved. It became clear that eventually, I would have to make a difficult choice.

— o —

It took five human years before Mama Lisa moved to the house—although she had visited regularly and spent time over, during which we enjoyed extraordinary adventures on our walks to the rivers. But she only was there for the first night of her moving in before she was stricken. My senses were clear about what had happened—Mama Lisa was in awful trouble with a large tumor crowding her brain cavity. I didn't particularly feel that her time was up, but if it hadn't been for Papa in her life, I venture to say it was a toss. It appeared to me then that she waited for a safe space to let go of her inner will to not fall to a seizure. Now I am certain.

— o —

The downfall with the landlady very much coincided with Mama Lisa's arrival and her following disabilities. Besides resenting having to take care of the property by herself, on top on no longer getting the attention she was used to, she deeply felt taken advantage of, which I must say, was unfortunate for her. But there was something else, something deeper and more subtle—even to the point of escaping her—it was how she had gotten inured to the intimacy that had grown between her and my Papa. Because of it, Mama Lisa turned out to be a threat of the first order.

It became all the more confusing when sentiments were sent on the wrong tracks, the emotional paths along which only humans travel. Resentment festered all the more as my Papa spent most of his time nurturing his partner's wounds and helping in her rehabilitation. Although Mama Lisa lost a lot, she gained in many respects; gains that brought her closer to the way the wild do their business. What she abandoned in human logic, she traded for instincts and a profound intuitive. Sadly, the landlady only saw her as a self-serving idiot.

— o —

All came down crashing when Fenderina met with her end. The landlady made Papa and Mama Lisa responsible for it, which in no uncertain terms meant that they had to move. I was not ready yet, and I went on

21

pretending that things could go into reversal, even though I had intuited much earlier that I would end up having to face a difficult choice—that of staying and never seeing my Papa again, or of leaving the paradise I had come to love so dearly.

Mama Lisa left first for the coast, which in cat geography translated as far beyond what could be imagined. Interestingly enough, a form of serenity resettled on the property, and months passed as if the old days had returned. I resumed with the exploring, assuming that my worries about leaving were over. My Papa and the landlady were friends again, and we all lived in Heaven on Earth.

Mama Lisa and Papa went back and forth visiting each other, keeping the three of us connected. It was all that was needed for a kitty to live a blissful existence.

— o —

The awakening happened with the winds that spoke. In the form of a near-imperceptible message that came from the coast, I sensed a disconnection—Mama Lisa was severing the tie that had kept us together all these years. My Papa and I were left holding the spiritual fort that had been our inner sanctum. Abruptly, I realized that I depended more on it than the routine sorties into a world I had become familiar with—the exploring was twofold—without and within. When, in turn, my Papa heeded the voice, he became distraught, wailing all night and avoiding food. His heart was broken, and to some great extent, mine became as well. I knew then that the choice had already been made. In reality, it wasn't as much a choice as it was a calling.

In spite of it all, I remembered the landlady as a kind woman whose heart had gone adrift. From where I stand in this glorious present, she is a mighty force with much love to share. My Papa knows it; that's why she will never truly leave his thoughts. I approve.

6 – THE LONG JOURNEY

Days, months, and years don't mean much to cats—and all wild species for that matter—except in the form of cycles around light and darkness, as well as the warmth and cold of seasons. The moon plays a great part in orienting us around time; besides that, we mostly roll with the rhythms. But I'm now in a place where knowledge is shared across many families of consciousness, and that is why I can converse in familiar terms. Of course, without my Papa, all would be futile.

So, about a month before the great journey, I saw familiar items disappear from the house. At first, because I wasn't necessarily interested in inert objects, it only came as a vague sense of space vacuity. But when I started having to fill the emptiness with *aspect memories*, I arrived at the acceptance that my Papa was taking his belongings away to an unknown place, since I could no longer trace their scents—scents that were mostly mine from ritually rubbing my cheeks against his things. So, in perspective, the markings of my territory disappeared in groups. At that point, I couldn't pretend that nothing was happening, as everything converged to a single point in time that existed in a very close future,

Part of me panicked, and the thought of taking off where I couldn't be found occurred to me. But it was short-lived, for without my Papa I felt incomplete.

On the very morning of our departure, with only a cat carrier in the middle of a totally empty space, I decided to stick around rather than doing my usual morning foraying into the landlady's garden, where she would be seen harvesting green beans an hour from *the now*. When my Papa firmly put me in the carrier, I didn't resist, instead I invested my full trust in him and the future, one which I intuited featured Mama Lisa.

— o —

As soon as we got inside the truck, my Papa opened the carrier's door so that I could be free to lie comfortably on a pile of covers behind him, next to a big window. From that exquisite vista point, I witnessed how incredibly vast the world in which we lived was. So overwhelmed and immensely stimulated was I, that my overloaded senses practically lifted me to a state of weightlessness. It was a magnificent high that made small work of all the previous exploring, a passive one at the body level, but charged beyond anything I could have imagined at a deeper one. My usually active self was hypnotized into a rare state of calmness; that is why when I sat between my Papa and Mama Lisa, during that session, the day following my passing, I expressed how much I had journeyed for a cat. It likely stemmed from my natural ability to cater to the explorer side of me—I was focused on all that we passed, as we rode along the endless river road, and later, up and down the mountains, to finally face the flat immensity of infinite waters. Other cats, I reckon, could just as easily have complained the whole way.

— o —

The high quickly dissipated as we entered an area of acute human activity, sending my instincts reeling. We had swapped the wild for something running counter to the natural flow. The air was acrid with alien scents, while a general low drone could be felt from beyond the noise of my Papa's truck. Although there were trees all around, great expanses of earth and grass were overtaken by structures and human housing. To that point, I hadn't been aware there existed more than a determined group of people; nothing in my previous environment had put me in touch with the notion that there were more beyond the limits of my perception. Well, I must confess that I envisioned other groups, but never in a precise sense, since it didn't concern the nature of my personal experience. But in that *now*, it did with ferocious vigor.

After my Papa put me back in the carrier, I was introduced to the small living unit sitting slightly below a street much too busy for my taste. I cannot say that I immediately hated the place, but I had my doubts as to the choice I had made. Luckily, Mama Lisa answered the door and things regained a modicum of normalcy.

The apartment was tiny compared to the mighty house my Papa had built on the landlady's property. It mattered not, because all I wanted to do, besides relieving myself and eating some, was to hide.

— o —

It took days before I dared peek through the crack of the rear door that opened onto the small deck. The world outside was menacing, with a vibrational reality that challenged all my senses. It was loaded with a foreign form of danger that came without thrill or the rewards of having accomplished something following exposure. It was danger for danger's sake, cold, brutal, and alienating. When I finally made it to the deck, it took me another week before I climbed down the stairs to the dry grassy area tucked in between our place and the adjacent dwellings. But the voice of the wild was nowhere to be heard, not in that anemic patch, or the sad, flowering bushes that lined one of its sides. I had fallen to the grip of a dilemma of extreme complexity.

I undeniably had made the right choice, for I recoiled at the notion of having been left behind with the landlady, but the trade-off was most mesmerizing. Joy had joined forces with misery, and I was left paralyzed in a tight spot between them. Time's rhythms no longer mattered.

— o —

The lesson, if one were to compare life to a classroom—not that cats know anything about classrooms, but I'm not just a cat anymore—was around getting closer to my relationship with my Papa and Mama Lisa, and to a lesser degree, to other humans in the neighborhood. All I had to do was relax my defenses and surrender to the reality of choice, thus solving the dilemma in question and gaining much in inner mobility.

One non-negotiable item though, was that I would never lose my wild side altogether; and for that, my Papa had to accept that if the new place lacked in wildness, I was there to introduce some back to it, via no other channel than my need to explore. In other words, I swapped alien danger for some recognizable one, which put me back center to my personal reality, and in charge of my universe. I was proud of what I had arrived at, and I can wage that it saved my life on numerous occasions.

Heeding the natural instincts is the one thing that keeps the cat a step ahead of all dangers, for after all, time and exploration erodes the alienness in all things. Simply put, I steadily became used to my new environment, and though I spent less time with my Papa, our bond grew all the stronger. Love and freedom is an alliance that cannot be broken—something humans apparently have a hard time recognizing.

— o —

The enemy, if I may indulge in the term, were the neighborhood cats. Never underestimate the viciousness of the common, domesticated feline. If told, their owners would never have believed what happened behind their backs. Domestication comes at a great cost, not only for cats, dogs, or birds, but, ironically, also for the humans who have accepted the tyranny of dogma. The true path is always the call of the heart—artists like my Papa know quite a bit about it. I venture to say that creating one's reality is artistry at work. I won't go as far as saying that those cats made unwise choices, but it is clear that choice dictates outcome, and for a cat to exist in the human shadow is to negate developmental authenticity.

Ambushes were frequent and frankly, they tired me. My style was in exploring the nature of encounter with countenance and purpose, to meet the unknown with aplomb—not claws. Luckily, those cats never were around too long; thus, they were soon forgotten.

At that point, I was mostly interested in discovering new power spots. Not only did I realize that they existed in abundance, but that they moved around as well. Based on a variety of reasons, these sympathetic fields grouped, de-grouped, and regrouped, shuffling their imprints as if integral to a breathing map. And so, when I found one, I spent the length of its tenancy as my dream spot, for it took me to the farthest places.

I wish my Papa would find one of them, so that we could spend some *sacred present* together in my new environment and much beyond—there are so many things I wish to show him.

I refer to that phase as the long journey, not just because it was a long drive to get to my new settings, but because what followed fundamentally amounted to travels within the makeup of my physical life, where dreams acted as the main channels of exploration. And thus, I visited fields upon fields, met with extraordinary beings whose energy radiated with unbound exuberance, all the while moving closer to the greater understanding of my purpose on Earth and the nature of my relationship with the physical, particularly my Papa. I so loved dreaming!

Allegorically speaking, one may say that I have now taken primary residence in the dream state.

7 – PERSPECTIVE

As strange as it may seem, I am technically a cat writing a book for the human reader. My assignment having been about understanding humanity, I only find it fitting to come up with an in-depth report as seen from the eyes of a unique perspective.

First of all, the wild are not as oblivious to your achievements as you may think, and the size of our brains does not disqualify us from having access to consciousness. I'll let you in on a forgotten fact: hardly anything is stored in the brain. For the sake of keeping it simple, it is mostly a processor, as well as a hub to connect to memory stored in the spatial environment.

Your deeds do not go unnoticed. No species wishes to ignore the damage to its habitat, or the carnage afflicted to its members. But neither does it desire to overlook the fundamental goodness that exists in every human heart, irrespective of the toll of dogma and repression. We, cats, are granted a unique access into the life of humans, where we can be as close to its core as we wish; although in reality, many of us suffer at the hand of distraction. To my credit, I rarely did.

— o —

I never had to analyze my Papa—he, Mama Lisa, and I functioned as a team. We worked of a contract based on compatibility and affinity, hence why the three of us connected the same year. There are no coincidences, only synchronistic events. "Coincidence" is a term coined by the disbeliever of harmony and purpose—just saying.

My primary role isn't to pass judgment on the human kind; only humans have the ability to show that level of criticism. I chose to be a cat because it allowed me to stay within the safety zone of neutrality. As in most species, I was incapable of conceptualizing on right and wrong. Actually, at the spirit stage where I presently am, there is no such thing; it is merely an intellectual construct based on the misleading notion that the physical is at the root of all existence—nothing could be further from reality.

No, my primary desire was to search for elements of the human psyche that could benefit my assignment; namely, establishing a heart connection with the purpose of studying it. For that, I embarked on finding a human specimen that could stretch a little, someone who could reinvent themselves based on private, unbiased observations. I understand it was a lot to ask, but the nature of contracts is such that no assignment is truly single-ended. I'm not saying that it never happens, but generally, there are sympathetic souls in need of partnership. Papa, Mama Lisa, and I were no strangers when we met sixteen years ago at the two rivers.

— o —

It is true that I said that I didn't study my Papa, but it doesn't mean that he wasn't observed, for I needed him as a channel for me to get to understand his species. I depended on his trust, love, and on him to provide the delicate balance of watching my back, while granting me ample room to do my things.

It is quite difficult to explain how I got to the human core while exploring the wild. Basically, it was contingent on the very nature of my relationship with my two human friends and selfless providers—I had to remain as much of a cat as possible. In other words, we had to be extremely close; yet, I couldn't exist in their shadow, for the colored lens of the human emotion would have tainted my perception and corrupted my work. Yes, *work*, even if it looked like play.

— o —

As I communicate from the standpoint of the *afterdeath*, with vast amounts of knowledge at my disposal, one wonders where Tunes, the cat, fits. After all, I obviously lacked the ability to speak, or form complex thoughts, on top of only possessing a rudimentary system of beliefs, if one could even call it that. But, for all intents and purposes, I am very much Tunes or the myriad other names still attached to my character; and yet, I am also something entirely different, as we all are, outside the limits of the physical.

There is, too, the irrefutable influence of my Papa that must be clarified. Inherently, our bond is such that it is unclear where the line that separates us is. It is his choice to portray me as an eloquent speaker, and it pleases me deeply, just as it did when he referred to me as Professor Tunes. It just shows how much he understands that there is something much greater to being than what plays on the stage of the material. Without his commitment to his personalized faith, this cat reality of mine would have fallen short of ending as it did, only partially accomplished, and obliging me to revisit your sphere to finish it, although, I am at a loss on how to explain that many scenarios have been played and

finalized across the many presents that you call time—
this one being my favorite and, by far, my most fulfilling.
Again I cannot stress enough that it took team work to get
there, as it will until my dear friends reach the end of their
useful lives.

Following my exit, I sensed for a moment that my
Papa had lost his taste for the physical, and that in a not
so remote probability, his sadness saw him to his last day.
It worried me somewhat, for I very much need him to stay
strong, healthy, loving, and joyful. It certainly would pain
me to witness the loss of the happiness that had warmed
my heart on so many occasions, and of course, it would
force me to rethink the soundness of my choice.
Everything is so intricately intertwined, that a slight
ripple carries with it the doing or undoing of entire
universes. In other words, my assignment could never be
complete if my Papa were to fall to distress. But, I rest
assured all is well by the simple fact we are still
connected in this very now. Melancholia would not allow
for it, even though many humans strongly believe it is the
way through which to connect with the deceased. There is
a fundamental difference between a connection with the
image of loss, and an unbreakable bond with the vitality
of the spirit. I shall leave it at that for the present.

— o —

It is likely that I will appear to contradict myself
on occasion—such is the nature of the *evolving present.*
Minor shifts are integral to the *breathing experience* and I
assure you they are quite necessary.

For example, if melancholia misses the point on
the nature of separation between the physical and the

afterlife, a touch of longing, on the other hand, helps towards the connection, for I, too, miss my Papa very much. It was in all the minute details that our bond was forged, the feeding ritual, the grooming, me waiting for him as he returned from his work—regardless of the time—and following him wherever he went on the property, the high fives, and the silly talk so fascinating by its measure of delivery—rhythm and flow.

— o —

One may be heard saying that the spirit of the deceased must be let go. It isn't up to the mourner to decide. If the spirit wishes to visit, it isn't necessarily at the cost of its freedom to move on. I, for a fact, am quite fond of the place on which I spent my last two years, for I consider it a realized promise from my Papa. That time was—and still is—purely magical. It also explains why my words grace these pages—but more as we go.

— o —

In perspective, the second phase of my life was an education difficult to negotiate. I felt alone—at times distressed—and I confess that I wasn't sure I wanted it to last. If it hadn't been for my Papa's hope of a better environment for the three of us, and how he assured me on so many occasions that he was going to make it happen, I doubt there would have been a phase three. I could also tell that he was just as unsettled as I was, and in a strange way, it made things better, or at least, more bearable. Well, I have to admit that I also drove my Papa and Mama Lisa to the edge of madness, but I couldn't help it. I just couldn't be cooped in, rain or shine; neither did I wish to be locked out. But my Papa was firm; on bad nights, or when intuition forewarned danger, I stayed in. In return, I made misery of their sleep. Besides jumping on and off the bed, I engaged in crying the torture out loud, mine and theirs, which called for measures that would eventually ground me, such as, "Shut the fuck up, Tunes!" That particular arrangement of words, for some reason, penetrated my core, turning my nervous system into the calm after the storm. It simply put me to sleep.

8 – EARLY PHASE TWO

All in all, the switch wasn't easy. Discovering that my natural world had been replaced by one mostly consisting of manmade materials, with the proverbial patch of landscaping gracing some entryways, yet depraved of the insects and the small lives that made the country abuzz with sounds, I resigned myself to accept my fate as the result of my choice to pursue what I had arranged upon arriving in the physical. I never had to think about it before, while living life in a spontaneous fashion, savoring it a minute at a time.

I cannot say that I pondered on my condition in human terms, but close enough, for there was certainly ample reflecting on my part. So, what was there in need of being explored that could bring balance back to the situation? I spoke earlier about introducing the wild to the picture, a concept that pleased me at the time, but even though said wild was within me as a creature born of feral parents along the restless waters of distant mountain streams, the genetics and memories were short of adequate against the vibratory and environmental onslaught of the city. The simple truth is that I was scared of a world that had turned into a compound aggressor, where danger came concurrently from all directions.

— o —

I arrived at recognizing soon enough that the dangers in question were in their alienness rather than their doings. Sure, there was the traffic on the street, but I started seeing it as more of an obstacle to negotiate than a sinister evil. Alienness is always forbidding, but unlike in the natural world where many elements of connectivity come into play, in the city, it presents a darker mystery bereft of the usual signals. In other words, the *artificial unknown* is made dangerous owing to its lack of premonitory voice. I didn't own the cognitive tool to turn it into a language I could first sense then decrypt; for that I needed cues from my Papa, someone familiar with the human mystery, albeit with a twist, since from my present perspective, it becomes clear that he, too, was grappling with that mystery.

In a way, it was for the better that we both lacked in human understanding, but I very much doubt his side came with the same abysmal depths mine was drawn to.

That being said, I anchored my hopes into our bond, as I slowly descended the metaphorical well of darkness, counting on him to not let go—he never did.

— o —

As I also mentioned, the neighborhood cats were mean. I reminded them too much of whence they came and what they betrayed—although I am saying this with understanding—and so, I represented a form of threat to their contract with humans. On some level, they envied me, on another, they relished my discomfort. But they weren't instrumental to my development, and thus became more of an inconsequential omnipresence than a focused part of my reality. The occasional scuffle was quickly forgotten, the patches of missing fur being the sole reminders. I had more important things to do than vying for the alpha position—I was on a mission.

As I slowly descended into the darkness, I realized that a diffused light followed me, making visible the things I couldn't see before. I am particularly speaking of my inner world, the emptiness attached to the mystery of my surroundings. Part of that semi-clarity came in spurts, like when my Papa encouraged me to follow him down that side road to the park at the bottom, a small park with a tiny creek running through it. At once, my eyes opened wide, my instincts propelling me up a tree in a display of unbound pleasure. There was still wilderness left close by—I was reborn!

There was also a voice flowing countercurrent to that joy, a message from a not so distant future that I tried to ignore, for it tainted my present with sadness. It let me know that all things were finite, and that meant the park.

— o —

Mama Lisa, Papa, and I walked down to the park regularly. It reminded me of our treks to the rivers at the landlady's property. There was gurgling, there were frogs, and many birds, including black crowned night-herons hiding under roofs of broken branches. On the downside, there were also people bringing their dogs, but Papa watched my back, quickly grabbing me to put me under his protection. I couldn't wander too far off for that reason, but it was better than I had expected.

In conjunction with the park, there were many areas of the students' compound that offered unique glimpses into lesser unknowns, such as under housing wherefrom I safely observed the outside's comings and goings. Among them, I found some of the power spots I spoke about earlier—the ways to the dreams.

The people traffic was intense as well as loud, and the car lot was abuzz with zippy driving, which nearly saw to my demise with unsettling regularity. It culminated in a rollercoaster of reflexes and emotions—the highs of the sacred dream spots against the dangers of returning from one of them to my loving provider's home. It took little time before I became immune to it—thus morphing into the proverbial Zen cat, levitating amid the chaos. It was nice, but some of my instincts were desensitized by it. It was a game of gains and losses that didn't amount to much learning; what it did mostly was increase the zone of separation between my Papa and I, which brought me closer to the door of forgetting about him as days went by—except, of course, on our walk to the little park. Nonetheless, some damage was steadily being felt.

— o —

Papa always served me the best of food—I loved the sound of the little cans of fish surrendering as he popped their lids open. But there was a black veil that hovered above my health as I gobbled the delicacy: the fish came from radioactive waters.

Perhaps it was a means for me to reconnect with the house, but the fact was that my kidneys were on fire and I lost all the fur around them, my bare skin sweating profusely.

It took no time for my Papa to connect the affliction with my diet—I never ate fish again from that day on. When panicked pet owners would have taken their cats to the vet, he opted to deal with it at the level of our connection, believing that the body knew best,

39

providing it was given the power to take care of business. And so, for the longest time, I stayed inside, taken care of, lovingly sponged along my sides from the incessant sweating, and also sleeping a lot, while being fed a diet of lamb, venison, and duck.

My fur eventually grew back, as my kidneys returned to relative normalcy. By then, I had little interest in resuming with my outside routine.

In the meanwhile and unbeknownst to me then, the park had become off-limit due to the construction of a new main road and numerous student lodgings. Nothing would ever be the same.

— o —

During the span of my convalescence, I slept on the bed, happy to be next to loved ones, feeling valued, validated all the way to my core. Papa and Mama Lisa gave me the chance to find my healing powers, which, in turn, benefited their own. I believe it was the point at which my Papa settled his choice of staying away from mainstream healthcare, which I find incredulous from where I stand, since he hadn't seen a doctor or taken pharmaceuticals in decades. He considered my recovery extraordinary in the face of the critical state he deemed I was in. As to me, I took it in strides, for love was all that mattered.

Did I almost die? I would have, had the conditions been depleted of love. But who doesn't want to stick around when there is plenty of it? As one may say, love is worth living for!

Which brings me to, "How does a cat repay for such generosity of heart?"

Well, it's already plenty tricky for me to ask, but I relish in the courage to provide the answer: a cat repays in trust, for trust is the ultimate gift for a feline to give. And to give unconditional trust, is to understand the fundamental nature of love. Love is trust—trust is love. It is also the nature of an unbreakable bond.

— o —

I already mentioned that my Papa and I bonded at first sight, but bonding comes in stages, until, ultimately, such a bond becomes irreversible. At that stage, two become one; or in our case, three became one. My illness provided the time for the elements of that bond to fuse and harden. There are no coincidences—the reasons were clear—everything was exactly where it belonged. It was truly a magical time.

— o —

I knew I was nearing full recovery when the urge to go out of the house made itself unbearable. I didn't want to, yet I viscerally craved to reconnect with the unknown, the explorations and discoveries, as well as some of the intoxicating dangers lurking at the bottom of that metaphorical well. My Papa was rejoiced at the new life emerging out of my being, but he kept an eye on how far I distanced myself from the house, often following me to make sure I didn't err beyond established boundaries. I couldn't always tell whether he could see me or not, but somehow, he was there when I crossed the line. Of course, nothing to do with the fish poisoning; rather, it all revolved around what preceded it.

41

I understood that Papa didn't think my environment was at all safe. I also soon discovered that the park had become jeopardized, and so went the prospects of my future night expeditions into it. Yes, you heard it; I used to sneak into the park at night, as well as the grounds of the old mill up the road, which, too, was being flattened by huge machines. As the well deepened, danger took on a new meaning. In fact, my Papa had been oblivious to my travels—at least, that was what I thought at the time. In reality, he prayed that I was safe, sending me on my adventures inside a golden bubble. I can almost hear his thoughts from this very *now*, "You're an adult cat, Mr. Tunes; I can't prevent you from doing what you must. Be safe, my sweet boy!"

I wish I could have better comprehended his commitment to not regiment me at the time, but it's not what cats do in the physical—comprehension is, for us, a living thing borne of a mix of sense-oriented experiences attached to their spiritual counterparts. There is no *middle cat*, no ego personality acting like an intellectual sifter. Comprehension is a state of immersion that requires no thoughts. But, again, from this standpoint, all things take on a different meaning. Had I been in a position to understand my Papa's entire making, my reasons to be there in the first place would have been devoid of purpose. And yet, I am there as well, keeping a metaphorical eye on sweet Mr. Tunes.

I never said it wasn't complex.

— o —

Next to the house, across a wall of blackberry bushes, lay a field covered with tall weeds. From inside it, it was easy to conceive that the city wasn't there. Mice abounded, appearing and disappearing in dizzying flickers. It was nearly impossible to catch them, so dense was the vegetation, but it was a lot of fun. Other cats wandered in there as well, but we were all too busy to bother daring each other. I spent many hours of day and night exploring that mysterious universe, and there was still much to discover when the machines came.

Our house was perched on a hill. From the rear deck, right in line with the field, the view took you all the way to the waters of the bay, and across to the three bridges that reached the big city in the distance. After the destruction of the field, a huge, dark-grey house emerged amid the tumult of tools, and rose to completely block that wonderful view. It seemed the world was steadily closing around us, taking away, one at a time, the few things that brought hope back into my life. With the park, the old abandoned mill, and the field, I had been able to recreate what was missing upon moving. With them gone, in addition to the incessant noise, I realized we were no longer wanted—our styles, speaking for the three of us, clashed too much with the ways of a changing world. I could read it in my Papa, as I also sensed it was starting to erode Mama Lisa's prevalent optimism. I so wanted for us to get away, yet, it never seemed to happen. In spite of my Papa's many promises to take us out of there, time passed and I soon resigned myself to accept a fate of non-fulfillment. My reality had lost its edge.

—— o ——

9 – LATER PHASE TWO

The razing of the old mill presaged change was on a mission. The construction of hundreds of student units announced that a monumental overhaul of our lives was unavoidable—either we adapted to the arrival of the hordes or we did something to save us from the tides.

Admittedly, I was in no position to think about such changes, although Mr. Tunes, the cat, was always connected to the *now* from within which I speak. In other words, I was intuitively informed of the unsettling future coming our way, and I acted accordingly.

Acting accordingly was of course very different from the way Papa and his partner defined the term. My version was leaning towards a less logistical strategy; it was all guttural—I simply teetered on the edge of bailing out of the neighborhood, leaving the past behind, bond and all.

— o —

My first move was to set camp behind the house across the street. The small yard was edged with flower beds, a few of them power spots; and so, I spent most of my time dreaming.

I did no longer care if Papa worried about me, although I knew he did. I was past owing anything to him, love or trust—I felt at peace with myself, cocooned within the *me*, sheltered from the outside world.

A few days within my escapade, I awoke looking up directly at my Papa, who had, against all odds, found my hideaway. I concluded it was useless to fight forces that I didn't comprehend. Actually, I was glad he lifted me up and brought me home—it made me feel wanted.

— o —

I always knew when I crossed the line, so I didn't mind staying inside for a while—it was part of the balance. I made it clear from the beginning that I couldn't completely go wild, same with domestication. I had to stay in to be out—and out to be in. It was a dilemma very much in line with the whole of physical reality, the continuous push/pull of opposites that purposes to explain we only are physical half of the time, even though the other half is only conceptually related to time. Anyway, the point here isn't to debate the science behind the physics, but, rather, to bring the worldly attributes of relationship closer to the heart.

On some level, I couldn't help pick up some of the human influence through my relationships; thus, as I sought to escape, the bond worked the reverse process of tightening. In simpler terms, abandoning my Papa was the worse thing I could ever do to myself and my assignment; it was defeatism at work, a form of self-deprecation that didn't exist in the wild.

— o —

In the wild, we don't look back; we don't miss what we leave behind—we know not to get attached, because we understand that if we don't keep moving, we either become prey, or, as predator, the prey knows where we are. There is always an element of finality that comes with attachments. They slow us down, they distract, and thus we need not spend precious time on enlivening the threads of our past. We exist in the *now*.

With domestication, we let go of the wild, shut off our instincts, and surrender our freedoms for the convenience of a certain comfort. Humans have done the same by trading their natural settings for words of promise, snake oil, and glitter. It is part of their specific evolutionary process, whether that proves to be a wise choice or not. With cats, I must say that the arrangement is more suitable; although, I believe most humans are nowhere near understanding why they are drawn to us. For one thing, we are not as selfish as they think; neither are we aloof for the sake of being mean. Let's just say that humans have their ways of seeing things through the colored lenses of their systems of beliefs, collective and personal—generally a combination of the two.

— o —

As I said earlier, I'm not here to praise or demonize the human trait. I only observed it from the standpoint of honoring my assignment; mainly of evaluating the condition of the relationship between two species, with the extra bonus of triggering into motion some of the most suitable attributes for the benefit of both. Of course, and again, the cat couldn't be aware of his work in human terms, but to him—the *me* of then—he recognized his purpose via his connection with the dream state. As Tunes, I loved dreaming; often linking the two worlds with myriad threads to the point at which they could easily become unrecognizable from each other; and when they did, I felt overwhelmed with awe. Much exploration was directly tied to the dream state. One may say that the physical is born of it in many suggestive ways, but I don't think one can scratch the surface of that meaning with mere words—it simply is. It's a quiet matter of one trusting their dream journey for the tools of vision and creation to become known, and then used.

— o —

I often, in subtle ways, encouraged my Papa to explore his dreams; even suggesting for us to meet there to work on the more sophisticated aspects of our contract. Although those encounters never were forgotten at my end, I had no indication he remembered them. My impression was that he was privately struggling with dream memory, in spite of his relentless trials—something to do with his overactive brain.

I imagine it is very frustrating to strive for remembrance and wake up with little to recount, especially when I know my Papa's dreams are vibrant since we meet often, even more so now that I have left the physical plane. Dreams are an essential part of healing, and much is accomplished when we get together. We aren't worried though, for we know his earthly self is tuned in, in spite of the poor *recountability*—he gets it.

— o —

There was one occasion, when he and I had what one may call a major clash—something to do with me having done something to enrage him. I don't think any of it was based in reason, for I barely recall the cause. He was so furious that I could feel the killer instincts in him, the out of control anger. I was very scared, confused; my trust in him betrayed by some incomprehensible evil. He violently kicked me out of the house, throwing something at me that could have killed me had he not missed. I ran the fastest I could, clear across the compound's parking lot into an adjacent property. I believed we were done.

But something rose out of my shattered self, a sense that, without him, my life had no meaning. I simply lay down and waited. When I saw him from across the lot, he looked at me, but instead of coming nearer, he sat on a curb, crying. I then realized that what was wrong with my Papa had nothing to do with me, or if it did, it was the sheer frustration of having failed at providing me with the kind of happiness I had found when we lived at the fork of the two rivers, a happiness he deemed he had taken away from me with the move. Of course, he couldn't see that it had also been my choice to come along.

I slowly walked towards him to sit within touching distance. My fear was gone, but my trust wasn't fully restored. He spoke to me in low, broken tones, which I understood clearly through the channels of the soul.

"Your Papa is very sorry, Mister Tunes, I don't know what is wrong with him; what he did is lamentable—you don't deserve any of it. I am ashamed of him."

Deep inside, I also felt sorry. I came closer, and then lay on his lap; something I adored doing when he worked on his computer, or when he ate. I loved him too much to deny us that moment of pure bliss. My heart melted as he scratched the back of my head. He spoke to me in a low whisper, picked me up and walked us back to the house. The fog had rolled in, the air was cold, it was night, but not just any night—somewhere, way up in the sky, beyond the veil, three stars shone brighter, flickering as if talking to each other.

— o —

The incident was a wake-up call for both of us—it tested our limits—but mostly, it revived the bond between us.

From my present standpoint, it is clear that I had arrived at a crossing. Essentially, my assignment was complete, but my Papa's wasn't, since it included honoring his promise of finding us a better place to live.

I don't purport to take credit for making things happen, but personal realities, when they meld, can find strengths in the least expected of places, mostly through better focus and consolidated powers. Such strengths often come with allies only reachable when one can open the right doors. I was in that place with my many accesses to the dream spots, taking Papa and Mama Lisa with me through corridors I had antecedently explored.

As our wishes intensified, so did the interests of those who aspired to elevate themselves through their private *learnings*. Seemingly out of the blue, the new home materialized, and the process of moving in manifested in record time—all obstacles had vanished.

10 – THE DEEPER REALITY

While it is relatively easy from my present platform to recall the various processes of my doings as Tunes, it is another matter entirely to reverse the focus and apply things from the physical standpoint. Tunes, as much as he was connected to me (his inner self, for short,) very much depended on the tight guidelines of his life on Earth to function. While the dream state provided him with many windows into fields of exploration, his body remained behind, protected by invisible shields. By that, I don't mean to undervalue the importance of the physical experience, for it comes with its many miracles; but guidelines in the sense that they are predetermined, although with the inclusion of all possible variations within them. Perceptively, the one most glaring limitation is the linearity of time and its relative connection to space, but the physics are irrelevant here. The point is that the physical has a distinct purpose with much impact on the spiritual, thus why focus and openness of mind are paramount to completing assignments.

I might also add that the guideline definition is open to reinterpretation.

— o —

All creatures of the physical sphere are there because of interest and purpose. There are no exceptions—we all are creators of our own, and only personal aspirations bring us to choose the path we take. All is choice, and once in the physical, choice is a measure of beliefs for humans, one of human impression for domesticated species, and one of immersion in the complexity of the natural world for the wild—with many overlapping gradients reflecting evolutionary markers. Again, the point isn't the science, but rather the nature of personal and group realities, and how the two interact.

In a nutshell, choice is the immutable factor that brings us to the heart of a most resonant dilemma—life itself.

— o —

But choice is only as good as the environment within which it exists. Without love—a word often maligned by fear, in human societies—the desire to live is practically nonexistent. Love was the reason I enjoyed a long life as Tunes, for the bond with my Papa was born of it. It is what kept me around when my assignment ended in the final months of phase two. With love comes exuberance, joy, awe, and the strength to override our moments of loss and pain.

In the wild, love is everywhere—it is the glue of balance. It exists as the law of attraction in the forming of encounters and events; it is the *magnetic conscious* that substantiates purpose into form in the physical, and into much exploring within the ever-expanding ethereality of the spiritual. Of course, it is difficult to associate love with nature's brutal side, but that's for the human mind to see through its own paradox.

And what environment do I speak of? How does one classify love as one?

In the physical, environment is defined by space, an ambience measured in distance and the time to go from one place to the next. Within, it is perceived as an immeasurable zone of qualities referred to as emotions, thoughts, projection and reception to and fro potentiality, impulses, and the myriad indescribable urges that precede our moves into the measurable. Love isn't one of them, yet it is at the base of most of those qualities. It is the *quantum foam* of all existence, indefinable by the human mind, yet present in all of us as the source of our very being, physical and not.

For humans, as well as the domesticated, it isn't common to delve into the paradox between this divine environment and the outcome of their deeds. It is just like saying that war comes out of love, that the savagery inflicted on the planet is an expression of it... Yet, those very deeds arise from it, albeit, with the distinction of being afflicted with gross misconceptions and a lack of foresight. They are the reflexes of the habitual, the blind acts of a carefully hidden system of preconceptions. In the wild, untethered from dogmas and invisible to the critical eye, life goes on thriving, unfretted by the notion of good and evil, or right and wrong.

— o —

A big part of my assignment was to not lose the thread between physical and spiritual—something that couldn't have happened in the wild, but I was to be around humans and their influence.

Being born of feral parents, on a farm, by a river, with mountains rising on both sides, and far away from any city was a good start. But I wasn't skittish, unlike Fender, so when my Papa came to pick me up, I was ready for the ride.

As I mentioned earlier, Papa, Mama Lisa, and I had entered into a contract. Because of their work in the field of spiritualism, they were very suited for the job of assisting me, while pursuing their own assignments; although, it could be said that there was a larger one that encompassed the three *(assignments)*.

For the sake of placement, said assignment is still going on, but on a very different plane. Tunes is gone from the physical field of perception, but he's still very much there in the all-inclusive present. He and his Papa can be seen sitting on the deck of the river house, or hanging out in the lovely yard of the latest residence... The field of perception, in the physical, is bound to a present *gliding* on a linear timeline, with the past in its back and a relatively unknown future ahead. It is a law of the deeper mechanics of the greater cosmos, but again, one in the image of a collectively enforced system of beliefs; by which I mean that the individual is quite capable of connecting with a more holistic vision if they wish. Papa and Mama Lisa certainly abide to a very different set of guidelines, constantly adjusting them as they go. In other words, they aren't tethered to fixed views.

When I say Tunes is doing this or that, I am referring to the part of me that enjoyed that long life in the physical, and to which I am still very much attached, for I am tied to personality; yet, as I have said, I am also a lot more. The same, of course, goes for everyone.

— o —

Since it is still part of my assignment to open access to the layers of communication between the human species and others, it is my responsibility to explain to the best of my abilities what kind of environment I am presently in, as well as the nature of my being.

For some, it will be nothing but rubbish. Actually, it will be of no interest to the vast majority. But for the few who have wandered along lesser-traveled paths, I am convinced my words will resonate at the deeper levels.

When I left my body, I was immediately overtaken with joy, a mixture of my own and the emanating nature of my surroundings, which to a great extent were also a reflection of my inner space—all this to say that inner and outer are simply the same. Primarily, I was rejoiced by a combination of timing and achievement. It's not that I necessarily knew when my time was up, but when I realized I wasn't going to survive my injuries, everything unraveled. Yes, it was there, written in the sand—the last call before the physical would lose its exuberance and the body would no longer permit me to explore my physical universe with unbound passion. It was the perfect timing, and I am so happy my Papa agrees with me!

But before I found myself in my new place, the instinct was to stay connected to the world I had severed ties with. It was how I saw my Papa pick me up from the sidewalk, across the street from where I lived in a daily bliss. It was how I felt his kisses on the back of my bleeding head and his hands under my chest and below my rear paws, like he always held me. That was how I saw him place my body inside a pillowcase—one on which he had laid his head while we dreamed of impossible places—and pick a branch from my favorite catnip bush and a rose from the last of my power spots, to accompany me to my grave. It was how I saw him, in tears, dig a deep hole next to the place I last waited for him—the brick steps to his music studio—where my body would be reclaimed by the earth that bore and nourished me. It also is how I see him cry as he types these very words, and hear him tell me how much he loves me, this dear Papa of mine.

— o —

There is an elaborate field of metaphysics in the world whence I came. It must be said that in many cases the teaching has significantly veered from the source. But not all of that knowledge has been tainted by dubious motives and gross misconceptions. There are true teachers out there and I am assured their voices are being heard. Mama Lisa and Papa hear them—why we got together in the first place.

The thing is that the teacher lies within the self, his or her voice readily available when the mind dares venture beyond the clutter. There may be guides or prophets, but those pass us, or join us on the dusty paths of our planned destinies—planned as in carefully scripted, yet unpredictable in their execution. Those timely strangers, beacons of remembrance, are soon to be gone on their unique travels, ironically, often forgotten.

It is unwise to confuse the prophet for the teacher, for the power of choice belongs to the self; hence, I am such a traveler to you, the reader. To my Papa, because of the powerful bond between us, I am the voice that he trusts as also being his own, for it is, and yet, it is mine, unique and sacred.

Much of the reality I inhabit will appear incomprehensible to the human mind, but not so to the

55

animal kingdom. There are many reasons for it, but for the sake of simplicity, let's just say the creator has become lost in his/her creation and is relinquishing powers to an outside force, having forgotten it is they that own and operate the tools.

The emergence of the belief system is particular to the human race; so is the field of philosophy. It may be said that the two parallel each other in a play of balance.

In the wild, the *actor* is cognizant of the source of their existence, for they see their environment as an all-encompassing oneness borne of it. Purpose isn't defined by backroom calculus, but as a distinct assignment birthed in a profound desire to explore the greater unknowns. By it, I mean that in time's terms, those very unknowns have not yet been created, solely existing as potential. In other words, exploring is a big part of the creating process, each stride an evolutionary step.

The belief system, as I have come to recognize it in humans, is a brilliant tool that aims at firming individual and social character. It is also an unfortunate model when such a tool becomes weaponized in the sense that it starts working against its initial purpose, thus disempowering the creator by building limiters, blinders, and then greater, practically invisible barriers. It is a form of indoctrination of the self, which aims at stratifying beliefs into reducing choice to an item of reflexivity. Thus is lost the original purpose.

— o —

One may ask what a cat knows about the workings of the human mind. Although it is true that I have a particular fondness for my role as Tunes, my various assignments have brought me very close to the human soul. I am not just referring to the deep bonds with my Papa and Mama Lisa, for I have existed—or should I say, I *exist*—in other forms, including the human one.

It is the compound knowledge of all my works that, as seen from the standpoint of this very present, allows the pen to scribe onto the virgin page. What better way to express my greater connection with the human soul than having my Papa write my story? But of course, the mind begs for the tangible, the verifiable. Yet, for the mind to find proof of the veracity of my words, it must reconnect with the source, for I am no longer of the physical. It calls upon faith to assist, but not my version of it. It also calls for a smidgen of curiosity, a need to see beyond artificial barriers into the unexplored. I know it sounds tricky, but the only way for the mind to validate my existence, is for the mind to trust that I exist. I can only affirm that I am.

It may seem that I have explained nothing, but I assert that much is being said.

— o —

And what of the incomprehensible reality I speak of? How can it be presented to the rational mind?

The mind only needs to imagine that such incomprehensibility exists, a world so alien that every notion of physicality does nothing but further its understanding.

So, imagine a space that isn't one, an ambience rather; and time that isn't time, but an all-encompassing present. But even then, the term *all-encompassing* implies a sense of space to the mind, thus it must be removed. And yet, instead of ending with nothing, one stumbles across infinite possibilities. In the end, we return to imagining, not a place, but a quality of existence that cannot be measured in terms of what we know, but of what we don't, which leaves the mind with an incommensurable void. But if one wanders down the path of the imaginary, one arrives closer to what I'm getting at; and if one seeks to become familiar with the dream state, one intuitively recognizes what it is that words cannot convey.

— o —

This attempt at explaining my deeper reality, and by extension, yours, is based in the work my Papa, his partner, and I have endeavored. I do not wish to take away from the magical being that *is* Tunes, for he will return to these pages for the length of phase three, although his life is inseparable from mine, as mine is from his, by which I mean there are no levels of value between us, and no degree of separation. I may venture to say that, in me, he is a fully awakened version of himself. He is the *me* in the flesh—I hope I am making myself clear.

It is also my attempt at describing the deeper meaning of my relationship with Papa and the powerful agent that is love.

It might be incomprehensible to some that a bond between two members of different species could be stronger than one between two individuals of the same, yet the scenario is common—it suffices to ask a cat or dog lover. Such query may not be received with a completely honest answer, for it is a tricky question, but there is no denying of the existence of these bonds.

The river landlady, for example, never pretended to love humans over her cats, for which she got my Papa's respect. Sometimes the truth is brutal and a level of callousness is necessary to express it.

Strong inter-species bonds have been around since the emergence of the physical. They are integral to it, an intrinsic *weavework* of moving energy through the *core spine* of evolution. Before taboos overtook the human belief system, such merging of souls, and dare I say, flesh, existed unimpeded. In modern Earth history, those bonds are overshadowed by the self-importance of man and his dominance over all that challenges his might. Love is regarded as weakness; hence, bonds are seen as the work of valor through sword and blood. When I say *man*, it is of course in the sense of a social imprint rather than a quality inherent to all men—I simply aim to highlight the *silent* beliefs that taint the social cloth.

Love is strength; expressing it is uplifting the soul that receives it. As rage is surrender, love is victory; it is bravery against the cowardice of hatred, and as I have said earlier, it is the glue that connects all the elements of the wild. Without love, the impetus to exist and create withers, reducible to the amorphousness of non-being. Lovelessness is a void without purpose—a state of absolute absence and lonesomeness of spirit.

No entity wishes for the alienation of complete oneness, a self with no others. Love is behind the ultimate act of freeing dreams from the shackles of introversion. Creation thus becomes the evolution of potential into infinite stages of making, failures and successes alike. If love is the source of existence, joy is its greatest reward, for there is nothing comparable to the energy that pushes behind it and the vitality with which it springs.

One may say that joy is born of coming into self-awareness and purposefulness, knowing that words do a poor job at shining a true light on the meaning of what it feels to come into one's own as a unit of consciousness.

For the sake of simplicity, the emergence of life is akin to awakening to a beautiful morning. For me as Tunes, it was a garden full of blooms; for Papa and Mama Lisa it is to find each other upon opening their eyes.

— o —

But of greater importance is to understand that the self creates his/her own reality, and that the world in which each of us lives is a unique version of what is thought to be a collectively accepted model. I am mainly speaking for Earth reality, but the same applies to all levels of existence. Reality is a misleading term, for it is the sum of all individual, group, and larger social ones, from the most minute of forms to the infinite cluster referred to as *All That Is* in the field of metaphysics.

— o —

Along love and joy, come trust, empathy, validation, beauty, thrust, curiosity, exhilaration, and above all, unimpeded clarity, a quality at the base of all communication, within and without. It is how we thrive and expand as a collective consciousness, on a path of no resistance, where play is the joy of work.

Oppositely, walking away from the naturalness of being is indeed an arduous road full of ambushes and devoid of joy. Play takes on the characteristics of pain and mischief, while work becomes hardship. Much energy is spent in undoing the creative, stalling evolution, and marring the beautiful.

It thus takes an ultimate effort for the creative mind to find the majestic among decay, lost beauty amid the scars, and light within darkness.

For humans, destruction is part of a self-imposed and unavoidable course into oblivion; in the natural world it is rebirth.

My point here is to make the distinction between the union of work and play, and their severing. In other words, it takes incommensurable amounts of energy to create from mistrust and cynicism, while it takes little from the standpoint of their opposites.

What I am trying to say to humans, here, is that their views of themselves and their reality are the direct byproducts of what they have come to individually and collectively believe, and the choices they've made.

I'm just a cat.

——— o ———

It was obvious, by the boxes being filled and taken out, that Papa and Mama Lisa's days at the students' compound were numbered.

For reasons alien to my nature, I began to feel overwhelmed with insecurities. What would I do if they left without me? Perhaps I had been too self-involved and strong-headed to merit their consideration. It is true that I demanded much of them, acting overly spoiled and downright aggressive when all they asked for was a peaceful night.

As a cat, I rode my moods like I did the weather, never victimized in my discomfort. The only expression resembling guilt was the realization that I might have gone too far at times; and thus, I would make amends by showing how much I appreciated being part of the team.

Things had changed though; my energy was more grounded, and as I mentioned earlier, I was, without truly knowing it, nearing completion of my assignment—I had come to a crossing that required making choices.

— o —

I vividly remember Papa taking pictures of me on the back deck. There was something eerily finite about it, a sense of end accompanied by the wish to remember a life together. I felt ill at ease, almost convinced that we were about to part. It could have been the perfect timing if something hadn't been missing. Oddly, I was overtaken with human-like emotions, and what was missing was my connection with my core and natural instincts. A layer of melancholia was setting in, my heart aching with anticipated loss, the loss of the love between me and my Papa. It wasn't real, yet it was overflowing with realism, at times, overbearing.

Not all was lost, as hopes soon rekindled the memory of my Papa's promise to take us to a better place. As it turned out, there was more love to share and days of bliss ahead.

It then all happened fast.

— o —

Unlike during the first move, when suspicion overshadowed the joy of being together with my loving *parents*, the passage to phase three was devoid of anxiety, at the exception of me being stuck in the cat carrier with Mama Lisa trying to soothe me, while conveying she didn't know how to open the door. Papa was still to arrive with boxes and furniture.

Eventually, I was free to explore the new environment. This time, I didn't hesitate to visit the outside, immediately acquainting myself with the sunny patio, garden, and most importantly, the catnip patch. And yes, there were trees to climb and a million hideaways in between blooming bushes, hedges, gigantic grasses, and outbuildings. I adored my new place then and there— finally, I was home!

— o —

Papa and Mama Lisa were also home. As a team, we had arrived at a place of rest where the soul could heal and the heart could beat to the tempo of life's rewards—steady and fulfilled.

The place was free of the angry or confused spirits of the in-between, incomplete entities born of existences that failed at bringing forth awareness. To the contrary, it was inhabited by myriad playful fairies that immediately took on liking us. To them, we were whom they had hoped for out of the many scenarios that stood before the selling of the house. When they called collectively for kindred spirits to heed their plea, the three of us heard, and with the help of our greater family of consciousness, we made it happen. All was synchronous. It was the best case scenario in the making, and as I said, it was fast, very fast—practically instantaneous.

Emphasize *instantaneous*.

— o —

Even though there is a specific chapter on the deeper reality, this whole writing is inherently about it, and thus references to it are inevitable. There is no point in extrapolating about my love of flowers, say, without the more profound ramifications that lead to it. The same goes for the entirety of my life as Tunes.

Phase three is the part that deals with the more tuned-in self, the one whose connection with the inner world is at its most acute. It is life for life's sake, expressed via much exploration of both the physical and the dream state, until the two practically become one.

It is also the part that most highlights how the three of us fit as a team and what brought us together in the first place. It is, additionally, the one most difficult to explain in the languages common to humans.

Phase three is a time/space that symbolizes resolve. It is what happens ahead of crossing into the next leg of our journey, what defines a completed assignment against unaccomplished goals. I have made that crossing—Papa and Mama Lisa will too when their time is up. I don't have to wait for them, since time is a construct—they are already there in many ways.

There is no in-between reality for us, the team. We are clear as to what our place in the physical is, what needs to be dealt with at the personal end, and about our contribution to the expansion of the *whole* via our conscious recounting and sharing of experience within what is best described as a class—hence, the assignment.

— o —

No assignment is ever imposed, yet it is one of responsibility towards the self. For that, in Earth's terms, it may be pleasant or downright miserable. At my end, *miserable* has nothing to do with the negative connotation it holds, for it is the intensity of the work that defines *value fulfillment*. In other words, persevering through adversity is preferred over lamentation and building a belief system aimed at justifying and furthering disempowerment. Unlike humans, cats have limited capacity for beliefs, and even that, I don't think the word can be measured beyond the de facto intellectualism of the human mind—cats react based on experiencing intense or repeated stimuli, but rarely in terms of value attached to such experience. It is neither good nor bad; it is to be courted, or avoided.

On some level, humans do the same, but there is a race attribute related to pride that distinguishes itself in furthering experience into diagnosing and labeling it with, may I say, unwise confidence. All it does is anesthetize the ability to swiftly adjust to changes—something unthinkable in the wild.

— o —

So, how do we end up going from the move to speaking of the belief system? When I wrote, "Emphasize *instantaneous*," I intended to explain.

There is nothing easy about buying a first house when the individual and social mindsets lean towards imagining all kinds of obstacles. Technically, it was unthinkable for the three of us to move into our new place, but Papa and Mama Lisa have learned to stay clear of the notion that the human, as well non-human, experience is limited to a *safe zone* moderated by what are essentially fears in the guise of an unverifiable authority. In other words, they kept on dreaming, trusting that a place would be calling somewhere; and when it did, nothing came in the way, because nothing was ever imagined to interfere. As a result, money manifested, the sellers were introduced through friends, a joyful and very skilled loan officer went out of her way to process the paperwork as swiftly as she could, and keys were handed over at the end of a mere thirteen-day escrow.

It is how, by relaxing fixed concepts, the inner channels of communication open—the bigger the opening, the faster and clearer the transfer of information. What happens on the surface, the paperwork, the logistics, the timing... is all contingent on the work performed at the deeper levels. For that matter, nothing exists without it.

Instantaneous may be an exaggeration of sort, but in the relative elasticity of time, thirteen days may happen in the blink of an eye. The point is that obstacles are the end result of the mind placing them there; to remove them requires the willingness and, often, the courage to change one's view of the self and its larger reality. For cats, choice is based on what's desirable and what isn't, and as far as the unknown goes, on an irresistible urge to explore.

— o —

This second move, not unlike the first one, was based on a desire to bring a better quality to life. It wasn't just hauling one's possessions from one place to the next, but also leaving a cluttered life behind—the clutter being of inner concerns rather than things, of course.

With the first move, because of our bond, I was deeply affected by the logistics of Papa and Mama Lisa living apart from each other. It's not that I thought about it, but there was a prevailing energy that tarnished my daily life, while presaging change. I chose to go, not to make my life better—it didn't—but to follow the love at the core of our contract. It didn't make my life worse either, for the notion of *better* or *worse* would imply surrendering to the definition of good and evil, which cats are incapable of conceiving. As with most species, we simply move on when conditions become undesirable.

The condition had become undesirable by the end of phase two; maybe not so much for Mama Lisa, but definitely for me and Papa. We both could tell how each other fared; him, with his creative soul squashed by an ever-tightening space and angst; me, with power spots disappearing at a critical rate, and deprived of vital exploration grounds. When, as I described earlier, our moment of head-butting came around, it was clear that the quality of life had deteriorated. It took that level of intensity for us to awaken to the realization that we had to work together.

I suppose it is unthinkable to some that humans could work in tandem with a member of another species to attain an end to a goal, but it is part of the universal reality. In seeking, not only the survival but the thriving of each species, we all have to work as a whole, for we are inseparable from the planet, and the larger cosmos that births us.

Although humanity may now be oblivious to the grounds, waters, and skies it treads, sails, and flies, it once humbly understood its place in their miracle. It isn't so for the wild, which can only exist as one with it. In a way, the human transcendence is the only way back to the source, yet it is a path of many self-made chimeras.

——— o ———

12 – PHASE THREE

Phase three was about a quality of life that was lost with the first move. The property wasn't the wilderness of the two rivers, but it stood as a haven amid urban reality. On my nights out, countless critters passed through as part of their regular routes to the next patch of green. Deer rested in the garden during the day, safe from traffic and view, to be gone as soon as darkness descended. Songbirds of all kinds nested in trees and bushes, until their young could fly, and bees buzzed endlessly amid herbs and blooms. It was a rare microcosm of activity, impervious to the sound of sirens and the roar of motorcycles. We all fell in love with it.

— o —

Although beauty and magic were paramount to the character of external life, there was another kind of quality that graced our inner world—love and everything borne of it. In other words, inner and outer existed as close mirror images attached to our shared assignment.

It is at times difficult to distinguish the physical from the spiritual when they exist in close parallels, and dreams from reality when they overlap. It is safe to say that the world we create reflects our skills—awareness being at their base. To blame the world we live in, as I have witnessed from my humble corner, for all the things that do not turn out as they should, is nothing short of full out negating the powers of the self. My point is, the more fitting the outside picture, the more likely the wellness of the assignment. This last phase was testament to the three of us excelling at the task.

Now, the use of the past tense is for the sake of placement, for it by no means indicates that things have come to an end. To the contrary, the work we share is timeless, and in a way, our urban haven is anywhere we want it to be, on Earth, in dreams, and the sphere within which I *speak* these words—an *energy space* between hearts.

— o —

So, in describing my experience there as Tunes, I am also referring to the work accomplished at my present end, as the two intertwine like harmonies in a song—a fitting comparison, since music was a big part of the life with my Papa. It is also fitting that my body should be buried right outside the steps to the studio, where I sat and often daydreamed during the creative work.

While on the subject, I loved the studio. It was the only enclosed place that didn't make me long for the outdoors. I was one with my Papa there—the ultimate power spot with access to the best dreams. I came in every night. Papa would let me on his lap, groom me while listening to songs in progress, often switching over to a movie when time allowed. Within the studio, there was no better place than his lap, a space where everything stopped to make room for complete bliss.

— o —

There were many corners to explore at the new house and I made sure to leave no stone unturned until I came full circle. By then, the old was ready to be revisited, and so it went, up to the point at which my curiosity was called to investigate further. I was aware my Papa had deemed the property a big-enough environment for a cat to thrive. I also knew that by breaking the boundaries, I was undermining his trust, but I couldn't resist taking a peek at what lay beyond the hedges and wood fences, and further, across the street into other yards. I was caught on many occasions, stunted in my quest by his unchallengeable firmness.

So, while I kept a low profile during the day, I capitalized on nighttime for my exploratory travels, courtesy the cat door that was always open.

One may wonder why my Papa kept that door unshut at night. It wasn't a test as much as he realized that I was an adult cat, deeming no human in their place to interfere with the wisdom of age. I admire him for that, for even though he rightfully guessed that I would follow my instincts to investigate the unknown, he couldn't take my freedom away from me. And so, in the night, right before his bedtime, while I hid from his sight, I would hear his words like a warm whisper, "Be safe, my boy!"

— o —

But he was correct to worry about me, for I abruptly learned what he meant by crossing the line. I had simply misconstrued where he came from, for I had assumed I was better equipped to categorize danger than he was. In fact he wasn't concerned about raccoons, skunks, or foxes, but rather about the one area he understood far better than I—the trickery of humans and their machines. After a night of heavy involvement with the neighborhood *ferals*, including the proverbial scratch fights, I found myself, in the morning, quite a way from our house, in the throes of the intoxicating sense of freedom that makes one insensitive to their larger reality. Before I had a chance to come to my senses, I was captured and taken away.

— o —

I was certain I had lost my Papa and Mama Lisa, as days and nights passed in the company of distressed animals, caged and stripped of my dignity. The ride had been long and scary—I felt utterly disoriented, my heart longing to return to the familiar. All the exploring in the world now stood in shreds against a despairing wish to lie on a warm lap or sleep in the catnip patch. With fear came a sense of humiliation. What was that thing with humans—that desire to take one's freedom away? It made so little sense at one end, but it was oh so clear in regard to the many warnings. I was in the midst of acute danger, yet I had failed at foreseeing it. I didn't feel good, plus my torn lip was still pulsing from the fight with the *ferals*.

I couldn't sleep—the lights were on all the time, adding to the overall alienness of my surroundings. Wailing, barking, and crying rose and fell in predictable waves of madness. It was a terrible place and the absolute worst time of my life, a time, as it passed, that proportionally weakened my desire to live.

— o —

When I saw my Papa and Mama Lisa walk towards my cage, I was overtaken with joy. There was something supernatural in their presence there, a feat that only the deepest of love could have made possible.

It was a long ride back to the house, full of stories and joyous banter—sounds deciphered through the inner senses mostly, but it was a good time to be alive again.

I was taken into the house in the carrier. My first impulse after being released was to aim for the cat door—a reflex that was as much related to curiosity as it was to habit. It was closed—I then clearly awoke to the now of my reality. As I have mentioned at the beginning of this writing, I was about to commence earning my freedom back. It made sense; it was time for a significant adjustment to our shared assignment.

The injury to my lower lip worsened. The pulsing turned to acute pain and I felt tired. I could tell Papa was worried, but cats do not think in terms of getting better or worse—it's all a state of being within the most suited scenario. It was obvious I had another few lessons to learn, in spite of having deemed this last phase to be one of pure enjoyment until my time was up. Had I missed on the larger picture? No, it was simply that we, the three of us, had amended the assignment to fulfill a greater purpose—something that had lingered in the realm of possibilities.

— o —

With necrosis edging its way to vulnerable areas, my chances of making it in the wild with that kind of injury were dismal. But I wasn't in the wild, so my Papa took me to the vet to have things looked over. My relationship with humans had soured since the abduction, and finding myself in the company of nurses did nothing to appease my sense of distrust. I fought them with all the wiggling my body could muster, preventing them from giving me shots. In utter frustration, they resigned themselves to just clean the wound and cut away the dead flesh—on some small scale, I felt victorious, although the large cone around my neck was weighty and made me bump into things.

Thankfully, my Papa and I were soon back in the safety of the house. He wasn't amused with the cone either—he knows a thing or two about dignity—so he tossed it in the trash.

For days, he took care of me. I slept a lot, often haunted by the later traumas. His generosity of heart was the best medicine anyone could have administered, rekindling, in the process, the fires under my subdued self. For it, I loved him back in ways alien to the wild.

— o —

Love is part of the makeup of the natural world. It is always present in everything. Humans close to it, whether culturally or holistically, feel it in their bones. But there is an extraordinary, philosophical side to love, which only humans possess, a quality that spills over into the heart of the species with which they coexist. That kind of love is an isolated version, the same way, say, a poem is a separate element of the real, not imagined, but manifested in an artistic sense. Unfortunately, there are also qualities attached to that expression of love that do not accurately represent what love is about, such as yearning for the unattainable or mourning an imagined loss... or, at the extreme, possessiveness and jealousy—all of them, excessive manifestations devoid of the joyful process. But, under the light of a noble heart, sadness can mix with joy into a perfect release. It is in its ability to give and receive that human love is at is highest potency, the version me and the wild are most interested in. As such, it becomes an active tool of creation—utterly unique in that it affords its user a taste of spiritual expression within the physical at a purely human level—something particularly difficult to describe. It would be like saying that man becomes a God in his own right without the recourse of the spiritual, knowing simultaneously that nothing ever excludes the spiritual. We all are, and I mean, all individuals of every species, subspecies, including plants, atoms, and subatomic particles, expressions of the spiritual, endowed with consciousness and purpose. In a nutshell, we all are creators, albeit with different *value experiences* as to the meaning of the task.

— o —

Human love, at its purest, is a *side mutation* of natural love, which, regardless of how far it strays, can never be disconnected from its source. If it were allowed to do so, it would take on a quality vastly unique, something akin to the properties of an instrument. Needless to say, its purpose would aim for just as vastly different ends.

But I am not here to talk about the excesses of human qualities, rather, about their behavior in line with the natural balance, and how they add on to it. Love for humans, as I understood it from my life with my Papa and Mama Lisa, rose from the spiritual humus to manifest as a singular property suited for the collective ego of the species. It could easily be mistaken for an art form if it were to exist for art's sake, but since it is at the base of art, it is best referred to as a sense-oriented quality. That love, though inherent, can be dispensed, shared, received, appreciated, and validated at the deductive/inductive levels of consciousness, while predominantly rooted in the emotional—and, dare I say—under the auspices of the belief system.

The point here is that beliefs are the primary instruments in the grand laboratory of the human experience. The self, either recognizing the space as its sole universe or as a room within a larger structure, determines the rigidity or adaptability of those instruments. The further point being how much of that organized system spills over in tandem with the love we share with humans, onto the zones of the animal world.

It takes more than the irrefutable, disruptive impact of the human footprint to change the inner makeups of a species. As denizens of the wild, they adapt, reorganize, but only to serve the indelible purpose of perpetuating the race; beyond that, there is little incentive to exist. But love is another matter altogether, and human empathy and generosity of heart is contagious—it is why those who exist in between, such as me as Tunes, thrive; and I trust that, through that love, remaining species will find their common ground.

— o —

Phase three is in essence the second part of this whole writing, a work shared between my Papa and me, with the support of Mama Lisa. We all understand that it will be received with the occasional *yeah, sure* of suspicion, but it won't change anything, because we cognate it isn't for everyone. That being said, I trust it *is* already resonating with the many whose nature it is to walk on the side of adventure.

When one believes their truth is above that of another, it only enforces all individual truths. In the wild, truth is like love—it simply is part of the makeup. A wolf cannot pretend to be a sheep for the sake of fooling *his* prey, and in that line, albeit on a more subtle level, no human lie can ever mask the truth. It is simply a choice to remain blind to deceit, and choice is always a measure of beliefs. In that regard, one may say that I am a construct of the writer—a *truth* I am in no position to challenge— but I am an integrated whole of my own vision, even when deemed an abstraction. The point is that life is a lot more involute than the social, religious, and scientific clockwork imagined by humans. The mechanics of existence has little to do with the way physics analyzes and maps material systems, for life is only minimally physical. Tunes exists within that sphere, but also as an energy gestalt without it. It is from such a place that I share his story.

— o —

I spent a year under strict outside supervision, while deprived of my beloved exploratory night outings. I begged to be let out after darkness, but to no avail. To relieve myself of my frustration, I took to singing. I enjoyed it quite a bit, for it soothed me, acting as a portal to sleep and dreams. All the while, I intuited my Papa was weighing in the pros and cons of extending my freedom. Finally, one evening, he allowed me to stay out until midnight—his regular bedtime. From then on, he carried me in, kissing me on the back of my neck and whispering loving words. I cherished those moments.

— o —

Perhaps now is a good time to draw a line under the fine nuances that separate Mr. T. from his larger self, as personified by me in this writing. Tunes, the cat, *is* and will always remain a distinct identity. He is such, as the *sum experience* borne of the innumerable presents and Daedalean variations that define his physical life. Because of his advancements through skills and keen intelligence with the assignment he shares with his Papa and his partner, Mama Lisa, we have *now* merged—thus, he is me as well. In simpler words, he is my creation; in more complex ones, he is his own. It is the nature of nuances to snake in and out of meaning, for they, often imperceptibly, straddle a space between the defined and the obscure. I don't mean to ascribe to feline sinuosity, but it is a particularly difficult item to extricate with solely the tool of language. It is a lot like attempting to define something that hasn't yet come to be, although I must say that the irony lies in the fact that there is no mystery about it, just an inexplicable urge to pretend it does not exist—therein breeds the mother of all deceit. Now, of course, I am speaking of the human experience as observed by me as Tunes, but also through the many channels of consciousness at my disposal.

One must understand that my words evade linearity, for they do not abide to the context of time, but they by no means lack continuity, since they tap into the multiplexity of gravitational information.

Knowledge defies time, even though it is common belief that it exists because of it. As a matter of perspective, knowledge precedes time and the birth of all living selves in the physical.

As Tunes, I was unable to formulate what is being told here, and for obvious reasons; but there is a lot to be said about *feel awareness*, or the condition of being in the there and now, fully tuned in. I was acting my part on the grand stage of physical reality, knowing wholeheartedly that I had a place to get back to at the end of the last act. The trick was to not get lost in the script, an item pretty much at the core of all assignments.

—— o ——

13 – INITIATION

By the time Tunes fetched the mouse in the tree cage at the river property, his Papa knew there was something quite special about his dear friend. So, when he started to call him Professor Tunes, it was clear he was addressing me as well. At that point Mr. T. had already aced the first part of his assignment, which was essentially to initiate contact at a certain level of consciousness within the physical. Getting Mama Lisa on the program was easy; she already had a foot on *this side* through her personal exploration of the self.

— o —

As I mentioned on a few occasions, the three of us are engaged in a contract whose purpose is to satisfy personal quests ahead of adding their rewards to the expansion of consciousness as a whole. Unlike a marriage of convenience, the assignment is based on true love—it was thus paramount that love should become ubiquitous to the daily environment of my life as Tunes. One may say that the success of the last part of this assignment rests on seamlessly linking two zones of reality, to which this writing is a critical part.

By personal quest, I mean that each of us contributes a key note to what can be interpreted as a perfect triad, yet as each note moves to the tone of experience, so does the chord. Following this music analogy, it could be said that songs are being written, sending their vibrational content into the universe.

When picking an assignment, we all choose a theme that best befits the nature of our indubitable individuality. It could be anything based on myriad factors, but it rarely strays from a lesson in need of being learned. The physical world, among other spheres of reality, is such a classroom, where the self is both the student and teacher—the teacher in each of us inspiring the student in others and vice versa—the central theme of the class being a study in consciousness, within which the belief system plays a most vital role. That goes for humans and other like-species throughout the galactic reality, although, at a broader level, the animal world follows a similar process along disparate guidelines.

I must stress that every word used in describing the nature of experience begs for a new layer of complexity to be included. I shall then leave it up to the self to explore the nature of personal choices and beliefs.

— o —

What is the character of our contract, and how did the three of us come into teaming up?

As I said before, we didn't meet by accident. I'm not implying that we had already worked together, but I'm not denying that a certain affinity existed between us either. We belong to the same family of consciousness and, as such, we have, in your terms, always been connected. The assignment in question formed itself along the lines of filling unanswered voids within the matrix of knowledge pertinent to our group, bringing that specific kinship within the scope of resolving the issue. As you may have guessed, it pertained to the nature of interspecies love and the human stigma. As I opted for the role of Mister Tunes, my companions projected their physical lives as Papa and Mama Lisa to fall in line with my arrival on the year two thousand and four, on the understanding it would take them all that time to get prepared for the encounter. In other words, they had other contracts to fulfill ahead of ours, although they were close and essential relatives.

The convergence of two thousand and four, as seen from the outside, barely registered as such, but to my Papa, Mama Lisa's reentry into his world was perceived as an oddity. For one thing, he had totally forgotten about her despite their prior if short-lived closeness, but one which by no means qualified as an item of forgetfulness. To this day, he marvels at how they weaved in and out of each other's memory, as if it had been meant for the both of them to disremember. The answers to it are still locked within him, but he guesses right by acknowledging there was purpose to it.

As to Mama Lisa, her presence on the landlady's property on that pivotal day wasn't unlike the culmination of a series of tumbles across a desert, where question marks, in lieu of cacti, punctuated the landscape. That was my first impression of her from my perspective—not that I knew anything about deserts and their flora.

But as she, too, had forgotten about Papa, it presented a glaring oddity at my end—they had been made to forget. It wasn't a question a cat would ever contemplate, but the acknowledgement was there all the same.

From my present standpoint, it is evident that the convergence was to exclude the clutter of close, past memories, if it were to start from a fresh platform. In other words, the probability of a continued relationship after their last meeting was denied, likely initiating a *sense memory* of something that happened elsewhere, and which in turn was indispensable in stimulating attraction at said convergence—a notion they both came to adopt. In fact, Papa and Mama Lisa had to forget about each other at yet a prior time, but the item is only peripheral to this writing. It is nonetheless important to highlight those two encounters as proverbial water tests, stepping stones ahead of the most desirable scenario for the successful completion of our shared assignment. The entire set of mechanics was well known to us from the inception, for it was the *stuff of dreams* before emerging into possibility— dream being the language through which *realizable potential* speaks to us.

I, as Tunes, immediately homed on the love between these two remarkable beings. It was a natural step following the fresh bond between me and my Papa— the team was officially created.

— o —

What *were* those voids within the matrix of knowledge and why *was* our attention drawn to them?

Our family of consciousness, as a whole and in time's terms, was behind the concept of physical reality. We dreamt of mountains before a single print was left in the mud. In fact, the ever-expanding galactic and microscopic realities are being dreamed of as we speak.

Although humans have taken a central place on Earth, they by no means are a superior species placed by a mythical figure above all others. They have unique capacities alien to most, but the same is true of the reverse. Self-awareness isn't patent to the species either, for it is the stuff of purpose, and as we know, purpose is in everything.

What is particular about humans is their use of the belief system, as it scripts the course of their individual and societal realities—most importantly, as it appears to function in reflexive rather than reflective mode. Our assignment was to isolate the cause of it at the level of the three, keeping a tab on the temperature of the bond, so to speak. For that, it was necessary for two species as well as two genders to interact for as long as it was possible, and in our case, it lasted for my entire lifetime—nothing short of a spectacular achievement.

Papa and Mama Lisa had to be particularly deft at confronting the nature of their belief systems, as they faced the challenges posed by those items skilled at hiding under the cover of others. They had to become observers of their own process before they could effectively free themselves from the enclave of the unseen. The assignment would have proved unrealizable without those first steps. They also had to be capable of recognizing me as both a subject of the wild and an equal member of the team. In other words, we were to meet half way, me by becoming familiar to various ways of domestication, them by understanding that it was unquestionably my choice. After those criteria were met, the three of us were in position to greet the nature of our partnership.

— o —

With the conditions to face the voids in the matrix met, it was essential to make the assignment part of living a regular life in the physical world. Outsiders as Papa and

Mama Lisa were, they didn't qualify as outcasts—their mild eccentricities fitting squarely within the remote social environment of mountain and river people.

Of course, calling a bit of awareness "eccentric" is otherworldly, but I have come to accept the human mind as its own contradiction. Again, as a cat, the nuance was mostly felt through the senses, since it affected my direct experience via the elements of domestication.

— o —

Domestication is the sum pattern of a peculiar contractual arrangement. At its base is a marriage of convenience that further branches into disparate categories. I am strictly referring to the principles of domestication, not the deeper bonds between humans and their pets.

Animals are primarily attracted to love as expressed through the offering of food or the touch of caring hands, but freedom remains at all times in the balance. Where domestication crosses the line is when freedom is removed from the equation. It takes a lot of love for a pet to part with their natural instincts, but when love is gradually removed, or downright denied, utter misery and sickness ensue.

— o —

Papa understood that a form of firmness was necessary to maintain the basic structure of domestication, but he also knew how to keep it balanced with ample servings of love. Mind you, there was so much freedom at the river property that I never felt stifled in my growth as a cat, but as soon as we moved to the city, the effects of domestication were strongly felt. At that point, it became extremely difficult for the three of us to steady the ground under our assignment.

Actually, steadying the ground was part of the job. To that point, it had been easy for me, as I lived an insouciant life, to almost take for granted the love that was given. As a matter of fact, I never presaged that my lifestyle would be strongly affected by the move, since my Papa was around. So, yes, while I leaned on our relationship for wellbeing, I not only failed at seeing how much it shaped my present, but also how quickly that present could be stripped of the illusion of permanence.

— o —

The point of all this is to highlight the nature of our assignment. It was above all a series of lessons that both enriched the self and satisfied the goal of the contract between the three of us. It was just as important for me to step out of the wild, as it was for Papa and Mama Lisa to get closer to it. Within that balance lay a clarity of being that opened the doors of consciousness, turning the life experience into a *lived-in observation* as opposed to the more common identification of the soul with its environment and state of happening.

It is clear that we were drawn to each other by common interest, but what is less so rests in the question, "To what purpose?" I mentioned earlier a void in the matrix, an item pertaining to the human ego that left gaping holes in the sustainability of the reality the three of us chose to inhabit. We were by no means forced to investigate, but the subject piqued our sense of curiosity as well as responsibility. We deemed ourselves responsible to diagnose the wellness of that reality based on whether its environment was still conducive to healing or falling into irreversible disarray.

Was the bond between the human race and the species it considered peripheral to its expansion still strong enough to steer the future away from dismissal, or was it for our family of consciousness to further invest in that version of reality a lost cause?

It may seem painful to face the thin margin of breathing room between two intense opposites such as *continuation* and *termination*—I assure you that not all experiments are meant to arrive at an end matching the goal, and sometimes for the better. So, in my present terms, the loss of a world is nothing more than forgetting about an item of lesser importance, although what has been lived remains very dear.

That being said, we still saw value in gauging the depths of the love bridging humanity to its source of existence. I was meant to represent that source in the context of our daily interaction, while the gauging was measured in levels of beneficial influence on each other. My Papa and I could have sufficed for the task, but the inclusion of the human feminine was deemed vital for a true evaluation, as the relationship between the sexes seemed to suffer from the same stigma as the interspecies one. In other words, the human male profile was subject to special scrutiny.

———— o ————

14 – PERSPECTIVES

Above all and for the sake of this writing, my name is Tunes.

Without my life as a cat, nothing of this would be deserving of purpose, the silent and essential component of this narrative.

My decomposing body is buried outside the door of this very room, yet I am also, if figuratively, lying on my Papa's lap as he types.

Forget syntactical trickery or the proverbial *fourth wall*, this is beyond playing games for the sake of intellectual manipulation; this is about channeling love, and also, loss and true pain; about tears and a deep sense of longing—it's about perception and crossing the virtual lines that separates worlds.

I miss my Papa and Mama Lisa as much as they miss me, which is proof to me that our assignment was a resounding success. Yes, there is plenty of love in this world of yours to propel healing into its most hidden recesses—so much so that my own kitty heart was overwhelmed by it.

I never felt the shackles of domestication, instead I proudly carried the wild with me wherever I went. I was free to find the power spots so necessary to my dream explorations. Everything had its place and I made sure no stone was left unturned. The difficult times carried no resentment, no judgment, no blame, and the hissy fits were quickly forgotten.

There is nothing easy about creating a life and living it, yet there is nothing more joyful when the mind and the heart work together through it. What applies to humans does so to all species, for we all come from the same biological stock and our aim is the same: to walk a complete existence, honoring our uniqueness. I have learned that humans are fundamentally good, even faced with a multiplicity of contradictions. Yes, it is true they have lost the ways of the wild, but it is also true that they are capable of overriding their handicaps and thrive individually and collectively. It was understood that our team was a fractal of a much larger model, thus our experiments and findings were tied to a whole that took on the shape of our work.

Even though it may appear that the magnitude of it is out of line with the lucubrations of a mere trio of unimportant individuals, I must counter that there is no such thing as unimportance when it relates to life and its many revolutions. Everything counts and everything leaves a mark; everything is and all events are vital to the expansion of the *all-encompassing*.

— o —

It was essential that the three of us knew our place as equals, for without equality there is no provision for team accomplishment.

It was a delight as a cat to be addressed with reverence and the understanding that there was more than just another pet behind those green eyes of mine. When my Papa said, "I see an entire galaxy in there, my boy!" my inner heart melted with incommensurable joy.

Equality means respect, trust, and validation at all levels, each an element of universal love. At the risk of repeating myself ad nauseam, love is the essence of life, plain and simple. So, it takes the ability and sometimes the courage to love, to recognize the power of equality. With it comes authenticity, or the capability to embrace all qualities equally, be they strengths or weaknesses.

Firmness was such a quality, with the peculiarity that it exposed both strength and weakness. Our assignment of meeting half-way came with specific guidelines that needed enforcing on and off; it was our individual responsibility to act when one of us crossed the line, something that amusingly came with equally shared errancy.

While Papa and Mama Lisa enforced the rules of agreed-upon domestication, I simply ignored them when said rules jeopardized my connection with the wild. And though it ultimately cost me my life as Tunes, I do not wish for it to have been otherwise; after all, it was the longest of many possible scenarios—there was too much clarity between us to require an extra lease on time to complete the physical end of our contract.

— o —

As I have previously mentioned, the assignment continues, be it through these words or the rippling effect of our shared work. It will go on unimpeded through resonance and attraction, as it is the case for all wishes attached to purpose, for all that strives to manifest has its special place in the *all-encompassing*.

Perspective is an elusive item that seeks its own center, that of being proprietary to its source of effusion, notably the self. That being said, perspectives can be joined without ever losing strength. It is such the case between Tunes, the physical, and me, Tunes, the inner self, or simply put, Tunes' spiritual extension. We all are, at all times, both physical and not, seamlessly pulsing in and out of realities.

Almost all species, at the exception of the human race, maintain an element of conscious communication with their spiritual counterpart; although conscious or not, that link cannot be broken without the consequence of the physical being snuffed out of existence. All this to simply say that denying the source of being only leads to a compulsive desire to recreate it—an abstraction at best.

Perspective as seen by Tunes, as well as Papa and Mama Lisa, was contingent on interaction with a specific environment. Similarly, as seen from the spiritual, it is a case of observing those interactions while living them, with the distinct difference that other events are also being observed and lived simultaneously, be they past, future, or seemingly unrelated.

In the instance of the assignment, it was only required of us to become active observers of our own process, something that was easier for me to do than for my two human friends—but they gloriously managed just in time for us to meet.

For the sake of utter simplification, I was Tunes up on Earth's stage, acting his assignment, while I watched, from the audience, a character rewriting my own script. The catch: I became a student of his performance.

I simply wish the same for Papa and Mama Lisa— although, as a matter of personal sooth, I believe they're doing quite well.

——— o ———

15 – ASSIGNMENT

In principal, the execution of the assignment was straight forward: live in harmony and learn from each other while exploring the layers of the self. There was nothing special about it—it didn't even require thinking.

What was different about it compared to, say, other assignments, was that we had to be cognizant of the work ahead and flexible in the way we faced the unknown as it came to light. It wasn't a matter of last second adjustments, but of initiation. We arrived prepared and ready to see to it to its end.

On my side, it was a challenge to not succumb to distraction at first, but I quickly gained focus and held to that clarity. For Papa and Mama Lisa, they had to remain alert to the near-imperceptible undercurrent shifts that sent the soul adrift.

The larger part of facing the unknown is to recognize that it's there, to acknowledge its subtle omnipresence in all the things we take for granted. In other words, it is the sum of what we hide from ourselves. The unknown is also the biggest foe of the established system of beliefs in humans, for it contains the stuff of inevitable change, therefore representing danger. Simply said, it requires a brave heart to foray into the darkness of the self in order to shed light onto the purpose of life.

By darkness, I don't mean evil—an interpretation of fear—but rather, the *unseen*.

The unseen is as much a measure of joy as it is of anything pertinent to being classified as unwanted by the self. The denying of love overshadows love; the fear of happiness cloisters it from happening; and on it goes. This is what my two human friends have to remain aware of with every minute lived, and at the time, it was at the base of everything we sought to accomplish.

— o —

Being observers of the process was only one of the qualities of being. It was operating placement, a state of non-assimilation for the sake of making assimilation more focused. We couldn't afford to be swayed by the currents of victimization, or stunted by an appearance of irremediable difficulty. Observation is taking into account all that is foreseeable with the aim of following the best case scenario, and all that is not, as part of what could suddenly bestow a change of course. In a nutshell, observing is akin to existing as the weather wane of personal experience. In this case, it affords the self to stay connected to the source of being.

I must stress that, as a cat, it was in my nature to operate close to my spiritual self, providing that I didn't stray too far from the wild. Oppositely, Papa and Mama Lisa had to work hard to distance themselves from the human locus in order to attain that perspective.

— o —

It touched me at a deep level to witness how much dedication Papa put in our bond. From Tunes standpoint, I perceived he saw me as his own child, someone to care for and protect. From where I stand now, I realize it was much more than a mere desire to shelter a life; he went beyond the call of duty in order to make himself available at all times by canceling all travel plans ad infinitum, effectively placing me ahead of friends and family. That was his choice, for nowhere in the assignment was he required to do so. Nonetheless, it didn't go unnoticed at my end—it was one good reason for me to patiently await his return when tragedy sent him and Mama Lisa on an unplanned journey. In the meantime, Fender, my sister, switched allegiance after deciding that the waiting wasn't for her. From that day on, she became one of the lives busying themselves in the distance of the landlady's house and garden. Her assignment was of a different sort, something in line with what any human would have expected of a cat, like leaping high in the air to catch bees and butterflies or staring at walls. In essence, she only wished to be a cat, although something untouchable preoccupied her most of the time. No-one will ever know.

— o —

The arrival of big Mocha was a jolt to my reality. Whereas the three of us lived in harmony, her presence was felt as dissonant, emitting frequencies high on the spectrum of fear. It didn't pain me that Papa saw in her a soul to be rescued, but I didn't think it was necessary of him to borrow out of our bond to cater to her needs.

With perspective, I can now see how essential it was for that love to be shared, and how beneficial it was to the assignment in the long run, for love can never be proprietary. It may appear as a paradox that I ended up loving my Papa even more for taking some of that love away from me, but just before Mocha died, stately in her newfound dignity and no longer fat, I realized that what I had deemed taken, had grown into multifold returns.

Finally, Mocha and I found solace in sharing the same dream spot, Papa and Mama Lisa's love seat.

— o —

In general terms, awareness is dependent on a healthy connection between the physical self and the inner one; although it is difficult to ascribe a fixed methodology to gauging its depths, for awareness isn't as much a measure of mental dexterity as it is of commonsense. In that line, absorbed information, as opposed to intrinsic knowledge, is of little use when it comes to defining awareness. Awareness is based in trust, the trust that one's existence has undeniable purpose. One needs not think about it—the wild doesn't—but one who cherishes every choice and move, lives closer to it than the mind that wanders the musty corridors of self-contemplation and intellectual rectitude.

In the case of Mama Lisa, who suffered a critical setback following the removal of a brain tumor, awareness was never challenged; if anything, her heightened ability to live in the moment was purgative of what encumbered her in regard to the assignment. As odd as it rings to say that the diminishment of a sharp intellect may be of benefit, such handicap is by no means as severe as a sound mind failing at recognizing its source of existence via the complexity of beliefs.

Out of Mama Lisa's impairment arose a wealth of intuitive skills, which Papa drew much admiration and inspiration from—proof that when one lives in the now, nothing is ever lost.

To me as Tunes, it translated as an easiness of living, a flow of the natural within human settings. The house my Papa built amid firs and oaks took on the aura of its surroundings. No longer cloistered from the wild, it radiated inwardly, a heart beating in rhythm with the passing of time.

— o —

By now it is clear the assignment was no critical mission, yet without it, we would be happening in a different present, one devoid of everything written so far. Such is the nature of probabilities, or in our case, plausible scripts.

I have mentioned earlier that the three of us existed in the best-case scenario; so, what defines a good one from a bad one?

For one thing, the notion of good and bad is of no merit here. "Best" refers to "most applicable" within the parameters of the belief system. Even in the wild, albeit to a subtler degree, *value experience* dictates the more suitable course to follow.

From their specific vantage points, all scenarios are of the best-case type, for they reflect the true nature of choice. From the overseer's standpoint on the other hand, all versions of experience are contemplated, thus freeing the belief system from its shackles and allowing choice to align with the greater awareness of the self.

— o —

As in our case, it fell on the power of choice to assume or not the observer's stance. To others, the nature of assignment takes on the colors of character, interest, and most importantly, personal evolution.

Personal evolution is the measure of where any individual sees themselves in any specific present. It is a personal evaluation, hence nothing of value in the general sense.

As a bit of advice from the wild, it is always the wiser to stay clear from comparisons. Anything that contributes to inflating or devaluing the self has no place in the mind and heart of an observer, whereas acknowledging the uniqueness of each soul allows the space and nourishment for the self to thrive.

— o —

For the sake of clarification, the role of observer is by no means a qualification. There are no observer families of consciousness, no responsibility that demands observing to be rule. In fact, roles and rules are hardly the mottos by which consciousness operates. To observe is to be willing to receive information from myriad sources and contemplate emergent patterns out of the resulting, ever-replenished pool of potential. It is akin to sitting back and gauging where the self stands in regard to experience before continuing. Nothing could be simpler, yet, when it comes down to personal reality, a major swath of humans struggles with the form. In the wild, it is simply acceptance of life, not resigned, but far from it—embraced.

— o —

Embraced is key. It is the fulcrum point at which life finds its vitality. It is the acceptance of purpose being everywhere, in everything. There is nothing that isn't meant to be, no soul regardless of big or small that doesn't have a unique place and a vital role in the makeup of all that exists. To embrace life is to feel all that is love and joy. Contrarily, to believe that life is too dark to deserve embracing is to deny love's entry into the heart. Love and joy have no counterparts, for hate and despair are strays from articles of projection. There are no ways around the power of beliefs—one is what one feeds the soul. Ultimately all converges on choice when it comes to seeking answers.

— o —

All of this writing is aimed at humans, of course, and it is why Tunes' life, as the lovely orange kitty, seems peripheral, but I assure you it isn't. Tunes is that very fulcrum point abovementioned; he is the love and joy, my model, my teacher, and one of my greatest physical achievements. Yet, at the risk of repeating myself, I am he.

Executing my part of the assignment, as a cat, didn't require the typical mental process rich in the pros and cons of particular choices. The natural observer in me took care of it. Simply put, I followed my instincts.

The thing about animal instincts is that they cannot be confused with the byproducts of beliefs, slow and unreliable processes of little value in the wild. I instead relied on an intrinsic trust in my universe to usher me towards the path of least resistance. Needless to say, focus was paramount, for when distraction interfered, trouble was never far behind.

Providing focus was my Papa's job. He was good at it in ways that not only realigned my compass, but also provided the necessary grounding rod that was lost in restlessness, for restless I was. Interestingly enough, a lot of that busy behavior was a display of independence. Out of his sight, I would just walk up to my favorite dream spot and sleep for an entire afternoon—something quite endearing from where I stand now. Of course, this Papa of mine saw clear through it.

— o —

In essence there was nothing in the assignment that took away from the humanity and felinity of our daily lives. We erred amid the better moments, anchored to a reality that, to a large part, defined our inner weather and seasons. Occasional storms blew through the harmony of the team, triggered by prickly moods and biology. It was integral to the package, warts and all, but what had been learnt couldn't be undone. Soon the clouds parted to make room for the healing quietude—for love to gather us back into its embrace.

What I am coming to is that individuals, as I have observed, haven't all lost the way of the wild, or at least, the ability to return to it. By that, I'm not saying that they must let go of their human characteristics; to the contrary, those traits are necessary ingredients to restoring the balance.

It is important to come to terms with the fact that nothing will ever be the same, even though nothing truly disappears; for what was, always is; and what will be has always been there. Yet, outside the time factor, the universe is in a state of continuous expansion. Simply said, a return to the old ways isn't an option—the assignment is about establishing new guidelines of cohabitation and assessing whether or not there is enough integrity left in the human race to achieve that goal. From my perspective, my time with Papa and Mama Lisa has clearly demonstrated that Earth and its species, as they stand, still have maneuvering room before the irreversible happens—we're confident there is one more fork in the road before that probability tumbles into its dark destiny.

— o —

When balance is reached, many species will have disappeared. Although it sounds like a heavy price to pay for humanity's recklessness, many came and went before humans emerged as their own, while others are merely at the early stages of conception. It is to say that there is a conditional time span attached to the emergence of any species, based on adaptability. Earth's environment can be downright hostile to some ill-conceived *experiments*, as it was the case with countless mythological creatures, and with changed conditions, those who had previously thrived are now jeopardized. Everything comes to an end, and not necessarily a disagreeable one. As I have stated before, only humans are attracted to blame. Without it, the exit of a species stands forever dignified.

But it is rare for a race to fall to its own doing. Ironically, it wouldn't be the first time for humanity, or a version of it, to stand at the gates of its demise. Entire civilizations came and left during the far greater than humanly imagined lifespan of Earth. When open to probabilities, that number becomes exponential, as for example, a nuclear holocaust laid waste on a parallel version of the early nineteen-sixties. But as we operate in the now of this reality, I must hence stay on track.

A fork in the road is allegory for the human desire to rectify the course from global unsustainability to renewability. It is no easy task in the face of overpopulation and greed; hence, the emergence of viral *aggressors* is to be expected. In a balanced reality, such pathogens would find their rightful place within various immune systems, but in one where collective, fear-based beliefs have driven the masses to making asinine decisions, the viral existence assumes the role of the culler.

As mentioned earlier, beliefs, private or global, dictate reality. It has, all along, been the choice of humans to end where they presently are—the aggressor isn't the virus, but the dogmatic mind. In that, even the science meant to advise and protect falls to its own contradictions. Fear is at the base of all human evils, yet it is a construct rooted in hypothesis, the imagined rather than the real—it is an illusion, an artifact of mass hypnosis. Only by removing the fear, is balance restored.

—— o ——

16 – THE PARADOX OF FEAR

It isn't my place to venture into the infinitely complex history and evolution of the human ego, but some basics are necessary here, since the question, "How have the members of the species come to fear their own minds, bodies, and environment?" must be posed.

The race, having evolved to the capacity of building out of their dreams, became automatically connected to the creative skills of *all that exists*. Coming into the awareness of the creator was twofold; it brought forth awe and a sense of limitlessness; not to be confused with the empowerment of the self to govern its own life. That new power was at the base of the emerging ego. In it, the mind envisioned the potential for incommensurable scenarios to unfold, and in that vision, it was for the first time exposed to the notion of right and wrong. Out of that dilemma arose the need for guidelines; thus, the belief system saw its roots tap into the fertile soil of infinite permutations.

At that time, the human psyche began to conceive icons in its own image—a straight line to the God complex and religions.

Emergent fear was the byproduct of incertitude around the temptation of exploring the alluring scenarios of *wrong*. Wrong as it stood was the proverbial apple, albeit without the biblical folklore. More precisely, it was the blank canvas on which to paint a human version of existence at the risk of seeing it unravel. In essence, there is nothing wrong in *wrong*, for the term stems from fear itself. The fear of the unraveling of life is the very cause of it. It is what led to the insanity of control, oppression, mass hypnosis, and of course, unjustifiable greed and wars. Tragically, for humanity, it led to social and individual empowerment hitting bare bottom, with the umbilical cord to its source of existence practically severed. Paradoxically, the race found its balance by investing in innovation and focusing those lost powers onto it. It is a case of the unraveling preventing the worst; in other words, a manner of saying that the unknown reality works in mysterious ways. Nonetheless, the loss of individual powers does little to remedy the inherent fears that linger, for relegating the natural *trust of being* to a projected, outside authority, is nothing short of giving credits to a stranger for the miracle of the self.

In a nutshell, humans would be better served by listening to their intuitive rather than the unchecked byproducts of their fears. In the meantime, investing in the bravery to confront the validity of these very fears would do much good to the aching soul.

— o —

By exercising force upon others, the ego effectively disempowers itself. It is one of the greatest paradoxes of mankind, one at the root of individual and mass madness, as seen through wars, out of control consumcrism, the annihilation of sustainability, and the irrational handling of epidemics. It is prevalent in the way humans manage social health, such as ignoring the far greater merits of proper nutrition over drugs, or the natural powers of the body to heal itself. The paradox of fear, as I see fit to refer to such madness, must be confronted before that one fork in the road opens ahead of irreversible damage. To say that time is of the essence in taking action is to overstate a glaring fact, yet I am ever so surprised, from where I stand, at how casually the race brings itself to the brink of collapse before it awakens from self-induced sleep.

As a cat, I cared little about humanity's doings and undoings; those were Papa and Mama Lisa's concerns. My primary role was to immerse myself in the love present within our communal life, bask in its intensity, and succumb wholeheartedly to the delicious safety of trust. The work of Tunes' senses was the data by which I gauged the depths of the bond between *the three of us*, as the emotional and intellectual work of my human partners is being monitored from similar personal standpoints.

I must reiterate that the team exists in both the physical and the deeper strata of consciousness; thus, regardless of where reference is taken, the three of us remain at the center of the narration. So, irrespectively of Tunes' passing, and in this very present, we are simultaneously straddling two distinct realities. Whether my words make sense or not, they are simply at the mercy of a limited language, while facing myriad beliefs concerning the nature of existence.

— o —

Disempowering the self is to force confinement upon its creative nature. Not only does it become blind to its source and purpose, but it also suffers moral and intellectual bankruptcy. At the mass level, it translates as political upheavals, fractionalism, dysfunctionality of social guidelines, and a loss of individual and group freedoms. With it, all that is good becomes maligned, and faulty rhetorics assume the role of truths.

I do not doubt that my words may instill a sense of hopelessness, but as I have previously inferred, the race is slow to come to the reality of its doings; thus, such emotion should come as no surprise. Yet, once caught within hopelessness, one's vision becomes so opaque to the reality of choice, that making reemergence into clear-headedness grows all the more challenging. It is thus the responsibility of those with unobstructed minds to show the way by example, a titanic task in the face of mass resistance—but it must be done.

— o —

I have said that humanity still had elbow room to maneuver its way out of trouble, and I meant it; but it cannot be done without a governing majority at the helm of the global vessel. Its people will have to heed the voice of reason and act on a conscious desire to save themselves from dismissal. In other words, a safe future will not accommodate the nonsense of the past, and at this conjuncture, I am convinced the race understands the meaning of what it entices.

Now, from the vantage point of the non-physical, multiple future scenarios are already in play, but it doesn't necessarily mean that their outcomes are set, since future and past affect each other just as much. If there is mental confusion around this seeming contradiction, it lies in the lack of understanding the significance of the all-encompassing present as containing the whole of experience. Simply put, both past and future are in the making on behalf of uncountable decisions made in multitudinous presents; thus establishing the greater universe as an impossibly complex infinitude of possibilities too deep for the human mind to comprehend. Although the concept that physical reality may not be all there is, and that beyond the limits of perception may lie utterly cryptic environments, might not be too convoluted for *man* to open to, for all that is required to unlatch the gates of acceptance and knowledge is some flexing of the belief system and shedding of the unnecessary ballast.

— o —

One may ask why I, a cat, would go to such lengths as to bringing the human mind closer to its own mechanics. The simple answer is that we're all invested in making the world we share a better place, in spite of the appearance of the contrary. The reminder is that, using the rule of average, the human soul is better and more informed every day; and perhaps, it is in that greater knowledge that what was previously unseen is now exposed. It is the human responsibility to assert value fulfillment to the evolution of the individual within collective endeavor, as well as to the evolution of the collective within the boundaries of the self. It must do so at the expense of letting go of bloated assumptions, greed, and self-aggrandizement. Only with a clear understanding of the nature of the self and the powers it holds, can the human soul find release from the contents of its own system of beliefs; items, which, like shackles, hold the soul captive to what amounts to little but a semblance of reality. Relatively speaking, routine, as in business as usual, devoid of the desire to explore, learn, and expand, isn't the model by which consciousness wishes to find its anchor. The idea behind the concept of physical life is to recognize the intricate details of individual and collective purpose through unrestrained exuberance. If the mind is inured to accept all that is *wrong* as the greater makeup of reality, no wonder it fails at observing the ubiquity of beauty and love everywhere. I am not saying that decay does not exist, but that, to varying degrees, it can be perceived as beautiful by the poetic mind. The arts, for example, have a way of seeing the *good* in the *bad*, and when one seeks to know why, it becomes clear that as soon as dogmas strive to tether themselves to them, the arts wither. It simply means that art is only open to interpretation, and that just like life, it cannot be confined. It is said that art imitates life, but in my circle, life is art. Following this analogy, the self can thus be compared to life's creator, and to the utmost extent, it is, for as beliefs change, so does the world around them.

— o —

I trust the time has come to say there is no God, no final judgment, no heavens or hells; just an unfashionable spiritual environment from which we all spring and in which we partake in pushing its *multiversal* boundaries—although the concept of space, here, is a misnomer for what is better defined as infinite potential.

It goes without further detailing that all that is thought as real, tangible, solid to the touch—all that forms the base of physical existence—is no more so than what seems real in the dream state. It is only through the belief system and the power of choice that humans accredit a greater consciousness for the making of their world, one in which they paradoxically see themselves as chosen, while asserting their central role through disassociation from other species and the responsibility of caring for their environment—nothing a greater consciousness would ever dream of asking of them.

— o —

Now, at the cost of contradicting myself, I by no means imply that believing in a higher authority is wrong. There is a quality called *authenticity* that pretty much overrides all that seeks to profile the belief system. *Faith* is another—by asserting a trust of the self for living by a particular group of well-attended beliefs. If a by-proxy method of empowerment is preferred, then a close intimacy with that choice is no doubt the road to authenticity.

The first course of self-empowerment is to own one's faiths. By "own," it is clear that I imply "curate." Unchecked beliefs are thus deemed dead weight, for they hold no value to self-empowerment. I cannot make myself more succinct by saying that the self has no grounds in moving its reality forward with only mere assumptions. On the other hand, forceful convictions can quickly turn to fanaticism, for they often come at the expense of greater truths buried deep within the self. By extension, the path to *authentic-living* can then be measured in terms of self-countenance and empathy—nothing that would ever take away from the exuberance of being.

— o —

In my contract with my human teammates, no deviance from authenticity went unchecked. It was paramount that awareness remained uncluttered by daily dramas, or in my case, distractions. As much as global reality is the product of mass choices and behavior, removing the focus from the inner process does nothing to induce change when change is needed. In other words, too much focus on errors leads to the arrestment of progress.

In our case, the focus was on exploring the inherent powers of the relationship, to extract wonderment out of every forward step, and humility out of those lost. As I have priorly mentioned, there was a lot of work to be done before we could meet, especially for Papa and Mama Lisa. It took the two, years to hone the necessary skills for what was to come. When faced with critical health decisions, they found extraordinary healing powers at their disposal. Years of investing trust in the body, mind, and their environment paid back in wondrous ways—they performed miracles. They recognized love's might against darkness, the light it shone over the cold of despair. They held hands when outside forces tried to break them apart and to this day, that bond has never faltered.

It took that amount of dedication to physical life for the three of us to delineate the depths of the assignment and attach the necessary value to its foreseeable outcomes. In the end, and irrespective of directions, we succeeded, and the world is a far better place because of it.

——— o ———

17 – CLARITY

If it reads like the team is taking credit for the betterment of global reality, it is misunderstanding the purpose of this writing. We all are individually in a place to claim our share for our contribution to the whole of existence. From the standpoint of the self, accomplishment is the best form of partaking in the forward thrust of *evo-creation*, a term loosely used by my Papa. In essence, it is in everyone's right to aver they are making the world a better place, if indeed their true aim is to do so. It is to say that to freely give and receive love is nothing short of achievement, and considering there is more love given than taken at any time of day, everyone can joyfully shout, "We are making the world a better place!"

— o —

Clarity of mind is key in determining the health of the thinking process. The authentic self is in no need of hiding, for, to it, there is nothing worth fearing that requires secrecy, or to an extreme—lies.

The authentic self trusts its place in existence and cherishes every moment. It doesn't mean that it is impervious to pain or sorrow, but it has learned to embrace reality in all of its forms, for it recognizes both pain and joy as sharing the same energy. In the wild, it takes much suffering before pain overtakes the joy of living, which, by association, brings the authentic self as close to its roots as any human soul will ever get.

It is in the clarity of thinking that the self finds its greater powers. Without the hurdles of beliefs acting in the shadow, universal energy flows freely through it, nourishing the roots of the creative with abundance.

From the standpoint of the wild, the concept of the self living outside its true nature is incomprehensible. Only a mind endowed with the powers of the creator can choose to misuse the gift and forget the giver. Such a mind exists within a paradox of its own making. Additionally, assigning a celestial singularity to the role of the creator does nothing but deepens the chasm.

Until the mind reconnects with its own creative forces, humanity will remain the captive of self-imposed boundaries and the notion that such limitations must be protected at all cost. Wars will keep on being fought, inequity will widen, while the natural environment and all its species will further recede. Yet, humans inherently recognize that such unsustainable conditions are arousing portentous winds.

— o —

Clarity is the antithesis of confusion. As contradictions stack up, powerlessness ensues. Seeking clarity, on the other hand, restores balance to the mind. But it requires mettle to see the need for change when conditions deteriorate. Unbelievably, vast portions of the human stock seem impervious to that kind of critical thinking. It thus can be said that those who live their entire physical existence on items of auto-induced hypnosis, become dead weight to social clarity. This is particularly tolling on the individual striving to empower the self, as a continuous barrage of disinformation seeks to instill doubt and undermine progressive thinking. In other terms, the staticity of dead weight doesn't exclude the ability to shout its slogans from the rooftops.

— o —

But it wasn't so long ago that I mentioned the power of beliefs and how the world was formed around them. It is indeed the responsibility of the self to seek clarity and carry on with its chosen reality.

It could be said that the self is made of many branches borne of directions taken at figurative crossroads. When a new choice counters and overrides an old belief, say, two realities, probable to each other, fork away onto their unique courses. Although it is relatively easy for the human mind to accept the concept of change along future lines, it is less so when confronted with the notion of an equally changing past. Reassuredly, I have spent a life with a Papa, who not only could relate, but also lived by it—an item essential to fulfilling his part of the assignment.

— o —

As a representative of the wild, I wage that none of its denizens are naturally inclined to connect with *modern man,* which isn't the same as saying that curiosity isn't there. To the contrary, humanity is being watched, but never with judgment passed, for the wild cannot blame or seek retribution, since it is empowered and ever-connected to its source. It wouldn't cost woman or man their humanity to wish for an intimate relationship with their roots—if anything, it would make them far better

112

humans. In effect, *the wild*, as a term, is a mental construct to imply a level of savagery to the natural world; a means for the race to identify itself as cultured and separate from the reality that cocoons it. That separation costs it in many ways, as it sees its environment as hostile and fodder to unjustifiable fears.

It might be of significance to point that the oppressors of masses, a relative few, endowed with political clout and vast fortunes, have invested interests in waging war against nature; thus showing no restraint in propagating falsehood through a barrage of logical ills.

Again, it is the responsibility of the self to see through such fallacies and, en masse, counter the currents of greed and social hypnosis.

— o —

As I have observed in my relationship with Papa, the path to clarity necessitates utter vigilance. Hidden, ancient beliefs continuously run in the background unchecked, often working against a need for change. The failure to confront them leads to much frustration and the undermining of fundamental trust in the self. Such beliefs can, to an extreme, create a personality of their own, leading to a total denial of the *true self.* It thus can be said that the human race, as a global gestalt, is afflicted with such a case of denial, which, if not addressed imminently, will cause its demise.

As I have said on a few occasions, the nature of my assignment, in collaboration with my two friends, was to assess whether or not this version of reality, with humans at its helm, was capable of correcting its course. It was an evaluation of the balance between two distinct factions, one quiet and the other rather loud; and to establish which one of the two represented the greater force.

It is clear that love prevails, but the joy of living is at a historical low, mostly due to the radicalization of uncertainty by unhinged spinners.

From this standpoint, it isn't a good time for the masses to bask in gullibility.

— o —

Presently, there is a great deal of attention aimed at a particular item of viral reality. If the wild could add a bewildered look to its observation, it would, for what it sees is a model of applied *disconnectivity*. Only humans have the ability to fear a hypothetical danger at the cost of overlooking a true one.

The systematic abandonment of the powers of the self, acted at a global level, lies behind the very definition of the term "pandemic." Many rational ways are used to enforce the need for the race to guard itself against its environment, but little is said about the fears that push for these extreme measures. As facts get replaced by factoids heavy on shock value but light on verifiability, intellects collide, while the direness of disconnection gets ignored.

Viruses cannot be defeated, they will mutate or go dormant, but eventually they will see to the end of their purpose, which, in a nutshell, is to weed out the weak and help the strong get stronger. They are integral to Earth's biology, thus running away from them only widens the gap between humanity and its source.

The self must come to terms with getting reacquainted with the body's healing powers as well as the potency of beliefs. It would be better served by walking away from dangerous chemicals in favor of a more holistic approach to healing. There are obvious parallels between the toxicity of some beliefs and that of pharmaceuticals. But again, fear is the great blinder.

— o —

Clarity is akin to limpid water—to seek it is to wish for the cleansing of the soul from the artifacts of distrust. Trust is at the base of all achievements and miracles; so, believe the cat when he says you should treat yourself to a large serving of self-trust and love—you well deserve it!

— o —

I have in these last chapters touched on the precariousness of present Earth conditions, at times tipping towards direness, at others, offering hope. This isn't a measure of my incertitude, for I am clear about the outcome of possibility; but if anything, this semblance of flip-flopping aims to highlight the limited options and the ticking of the clock. When I say there is one more fork in the road, I mean that it must be taken for this version of humanity to see many more sunrises. In the end, as in the beginning, it all hinges on choice—individual and collective. It is the purpose of humanity to attain the skill level to master the tools it has earned through many achievements. To fall to the folly of straying from that mission is akin to global suicide, translating as a critical failure at the spiritual end. If it were to so happen, it would be of no consequence to consciousness at large, but

115

for those like myself who invested much energy in the concept of the physical, it would leave its mark; mind you, not necessarily in the form of nostalgia, for such failures predictably happen, as they have with other versions of Earth and its greater cosmos. Only the nature of the assignment ties me intimately to the present reality. Soon, and in time's terms, Papa and Mama Lisa will join me to a place where we can reminisce about a life shared together, a play that unraveled as scripted, but whose end remained purposely unwritten.

18 – MY NAME IS TUNES

My name is Tunes and, today, I miss my Papa and Mama Lisa very much. I miss the dream circles of the garden, the big Japanese maple tree, the roses, the catnip patch, and the voices across the hedge. I miss the magic of music emanating from the studio and the daily rituals of food, grooming, petting, and kisses... I miss the human love, the human touch, the sense of safety inside the home—the smells, the warm glow of room lights when it was dark and wet outside. I miss sleeping on the bed, and the myriad comfy corners of the house. I miss my Papa's lap while he and Mama Lisa watched movies together, or after they finished eating at the big table. I miss the mornings when we all got up together, ready for new adventures. I miss the big summer moon and the nights of exploration, the unknown behind every moment and prop—I miss my entire life with that dear Papa of mine... I pine for songbirds circling above me, for the visiting deer on his day of rest, and for all the wildlife passing through, oblivious to urban reality, walking the paths of years long gone, like ghosts straddling the many nows of time.

—o—

I lived a blessed life, one full of spontaneous outbreaks of joy. I wasn't quite the wild, but rather the wild within the tamed, a place that suited me well.

If I am bringing forth these earthly emotions, it is because they mean much to me, for irrespectively of what was said before, no part of experience is ever discarded to the bins of disremembrance. If it isn't nostalgia speaking, it is hence a quality of joy berthed in the awareness that all times and events are forever present, alive, and, to a delightful extent, in a state of change without ever losing their unique signatures. It is in revisiting these places that I relish, in minute details, the scents, the buzz of a bee, the golden glow of love as it moves around our little world. Time might have taken me away from my Papa and Mama Lisa's love, but I am never far from love and the hearts from which it radiates. I am always there when such words as, *I love you, Mr. Tunes* are spoken, or when Mama Lisa, in a delicious moment, forgets that I am no longer sleeping amid the blooms. Those reconnections at the subtle level, so alive, so full of vitality, are as real as real gets, for in this very now, there is a hand stroking the back of my neck and the warmth of a lap below me, while the tapping of keys gently takes me into a world of dreams.

— o —

Early in this writing I mentioned how much I loved dreaming—as in the act of being fully present in the dream state. The dream experience is the exploration of possibilities in endless permutations; it is akin to an encounter with a glorious unknown where the elements of its making ring of the familiar.

One could loosely say that we dream of worlds ahead of their manifestation. It is a sphere of experiment and conception at the heightened *bliss levels* of the soul. It is also a meeting place between layers of reality. But to say that dreams are precursors of reality is to misconstrue the reality of dreams. From my standpoint, as Tunes, dreams were worlds upon worlds of magical adventures, which, tied to my daily waking self, amounted to a complete experience. Dreaming was not an escape into other universes, but rather the exploration of an inextricable sublayer of the physical environment, as well as that of many probable realities and numerous non-physical ones. Suffice to say that to me, as a cat, the joy was in completely immersing myself in the dream, fully aware, and coming out of it with my senses resonating sympathetically with the physical.

There is nothing remotely empirical about reflecting on my dream experience, for it is part of the private journey, a subjective happening based on the auspicious convergence of personal traits and interests.

— o —

The aim of this chapter is to clarify the seeming gaps between Tunes, the cat; Tunes, the spirit; and finally, Tunes' inner self. It is obvious that none of this writing, which can only exist in collaboration with my Papa's pen, is coming directly from the lovely orange kitty, the magical being, whose experience ended with his physical death.

It is thus natural to orient the focus to the spiritual side whence this material emerges; the first question being who's the one doing the talking, and how does it get to the page.

Not knowing how to formulate the answer in advance might prove tricky, but I trust the wording will flow unimpeded.

Tunes, the spirit, is the in-between identity that connects with my beloved Papa through the private channels of our inseparable connection. For that, it is required of him (Papa) to not interfere using the mental process, and above all, to trust that the words coming out of his fingers are not the byproducts of his wild imaginings. I can wage to the reality of his doubts, but he is quite aware of his choice to go with the procedure. It is, after all, part of his assignment to utilize his unique skills in equally unique ways.

(On a side note, it makes zero difference whether this material is perceived as imaginary or not; what matters is that it is given a chance to grace these pages.)

— o —

In essence, I am Tunes' inner self, tailored to sit closest to my earthly experience, while my *oversoul* watches over. There is nothing to it, and as the verb "tailor" indicates, it is a simple change of clothes to fit the occasion.

Of course, from the standpoint of Tunes, the cat, I was, in time's terms, far from reflecting on the various levels of my being, for there was a world to explore. It is the same with Papa and Mama Lisa, who are dealing with a reality that demands their focus. So, in a purely analogical sense, the physical experience is quite similar to being onstage, where the actor cannot afford to lose their grip on the reality of the play. But at no time does that actor come loose off the self, and, as Tunes, I never was very far from my deeper ties. To that effect, no human is ever so distant either from their source as to become fully disconnected, for life couldn't be sustained. Although, the fact remains that the human ego has strayed from its natural path and must at some point return to the fold of its fundamental reason of being; a point which I believe has been emphasized enough along these pages.

The divisions of the self are to a large extent the construct of the intellect—a redundancy if I may say—for the mind is berthed at the very center of its larger reality. To treat it as a separate part of the whole is to negate its greater potential, as well as the wealth of resources at its disposal. In the wild, that connection with the deep self translates as an instinctual reality enjoined by the tools of survival—and a vivid, sense-oriented appreciation of experience. In humans, it comes in the form of personal and collective achievements in the arts, philosophy, science, and social endeavor.

There are no such divisions as to label the larger gestalt of the self by layers. Loosely put, each *platform experience* is the end-work of a larger purpose; but that still fails at recognizing the all-ambient reality of purpose. Yes, it could be said that the whole is made of parts, but at no time need these parts become entirely independent from a whole greater than their sum. It could also be said that each of the parts is endowed with a fractal of the whole, and thus cognizant of its undeniable potential for expansion. In that respect, the wild is fully aware of its purpose.

— o —

When I say that I miss my Papa, I do from the standpoint of the extraordinary life of an orange kitty born by a river snaking amid mountains. The loss is his feeling; the longing, a profound recognition of his sixteen precious years of life as his Papa's companion. These feelings are mine too, as well as those of the oversoul, each translated in the terms of our respective realities. Yet, each of these emotions, irrespective of the angle of perception, remains one and the same.

There are too many permutations involved in gauging the wholeness of these qualities of being—within the greater self—to come up with a picture clear enough for the human mind to grasp, but I am certain that those who have come this far, intrinsically know what I am saying, for they have arrived at the understanding of the nature of their personal existence.

— o —

The oversoul—a term borrowed from the world of metaphysics for short of a substitution—is where the inspiration for most of this material stems from. It is a place of greater knowledge, where creative forces churn realities in bursts of unbridled exuberance. It is also an *ambient space* where my Papa and I exist as one, albeit without saying that we are one; and yet we are—and yet we're not. In that reality, the one from which I now report, I am, figuratively-speaking, Professor Tunes, but I go by many other names, depending on what connection is established. I can be a female or male figure, a human or animal one, or none at all.

Tunes is an endearing creature, a sacred being I am quite fond of. It is thus in his name that I allow a glimpse of my *thoughtscape* to wander into his former world, for it is his wish, his statement of love and unbound appreciation for a life of bliss and achievement. Each and every word on these pages is testament to his commitment to his assignment—one far from ended—for he, his Papa, and Mama Lisa have much to look for in the many nooks of consciousness—many adventures, many creations to tend to, and much love to share.

It goes without saying that I wouldn't be here if that Papa of his hadn't looked in his eyes that one day and whispered, *"There is an entire universe in there, my boy."*

— o —

So yes, I am known as Tunes—the cat, the spirit, and the soul. I spring from the same consciousness whence you came, you, the men and women I met on the many paths of my explorations, at times our roles reversed, you, the wild, I, the captive of my thoughts. We met at the multitudinous resting places of the traveling soul, recounting a story or two before moving on. Of equal race, we wed, or were pushed away by the counter-forces of attraction. As different, we enjoined, or might have fought to the death—it is all part of experience, the good and the bad, for consciousness judges not, thriving instead on the unpolarized intensity of experience.

I am Tunes among many names; blessed to remain so tightly connected to my two human partners; honored to be alive and welcome in a reality that is no longer mine to enjoy in the flesh, but whose many presents vividly resonate with the now of the *beyonddeath*.

As Tunes, I roam the memory lanes of the familiar, pathways as tangible as those of the physical. I visit the places my Papa and I once shared—at times different, at others, the same. We sit together on the porch of the old house, or walk the leaf-covered trail that leads to the confluence of the two rivers. I sometimes wait behind the studio door, next to my buried bones, knowing there is love amid the playing, and many thoughts cast my way. I have said it before and will say it once again, "I am never too far from love." And thus love will ever be near, within and without the continuum of time and space.

— o —

My Papa and I met at the merging of two exploratory paths, at the onset of eons passed. It could be said the Earth was young, but it was in fact very old, for it had already seen futures in a multiplicity of forms. Time takes us to its many nows, either at once or in flows. Forward, backward, upward, and sideway we go. It suffices to imagine a world to find oneself within, for within is the outer space of the creator. Dreams are borne of purpose and purpose of dreams. Papa, Mama Lisa, and I stand on a high mesa overlooking the vast plane of existence. We don't wish the company of others quite yet, although they are around, old and new friends throughout the spaces of time, some the creations, some the creators, teachers and learners in no particular order. We are the dreamers as well as the builders, and when the winds blow down the walls of our edifices, we raise new ones through which the currents can flow unimpeded, while inside, the pages gently turn.

It is in the inner world, where *all* is, that we garner the mighty forces of our birth in the physical. All of us, the humans and the wild, empowered to test our skills, we emerge from the warm wombs of mothers into the dawn of life, till dusk sees us through the gates of *the wherefrom* we originally came.

As Tunes, the spirit, I favor the sound and poetry of words—they carry voices beyond mere meaning—for the tongues of *man* come short of forth-bringing the notion of worlds without speech. There is language everywhere though, carried in myriad magnetic currents, within and outside the physical realm. When one listens closely, with all their senses and intuitive skills tuned to past the clutter of everyday thoughts, the walls between realities one by one disappear. And thus, material Earth is no longer seen as such, but as the radiating orb of its spiritual self, with all things connected and pulsing—all the tones, colors, and the full spectrum of vibrational existence, settling into rhythms and forms.

From that place, the vision of man and woman becomes that of the wild, no longer an image received, but also one sent, for the eye now belongs as much to the spirit as it does to the flesh.

— o —

As to Tunes, the orange feline, he lives forever in a blissed state of being, for he is now free from the enclave of time. His body has returned to the earth, a place the flesh longs to reconnect with when the spirit must depart. Although it appears that severance is made between the material and the ethereal realms, the essence of life remains within every cell organism, every molecule, atom, subatomic particle, wave, and the myriad units of consciousness carrying out their work out of their unique characteristics and purpose.

One of the greatest human errors is to fail to ascribe consciousness to all participants in the physical experiment. The brain, without specialized awareness present within the minutest components of the body, is incapable of recognizing purpose; and thus in no right to exist in the first place. The failure to admit to the powers of the body, or worse, the act of demonizing the flesh in the face of its relentless drive to heal the ills forced upon it is most unfortunate. The body as well as the entire physical universe aren't simply sets of components accidentally thrust upon organized existence by powers borne of the inevitable mergence of nothing into something; the desire to create and be realized at all levels prevails over all unfinished scientific and religious concepts and constructs. In other words, the world unconditionally *is*, in spite of all the ways it might be intellectually interpreted. In that respect, the wild holds a distinct advantage over the civilized, for it exists in full synchrony with its environment, unimpeded by the ballast of dogmas and unchecked beliefs.

— o —

To return to the orange kitty, let it be said that he is aware of this writing through connective resonance. My words are his, albeit in the form of sense-oriented interpretive patterns. As previously mentioned, all which is love is never too far from him. And so, it isn't unusual that he should find himself sleeping on his Papa's lap during the course of this dictation. After all, he slept cozily in that spot through the making of the many books written before this.

My name is Tunes and it is time to say goodbye.

— o —

THE END
IS
THE BEGINNING

PREVIOUS WORKS
BY THE AUTHOR

- **The Disappearance of Olaf Swyndle** © 2016
  An Improbable Emergence – Book 1

- **The Hektor Dilemma** © 2016
  An Improbable emergence – Book 2

- **Ma-I's Grand Gathering** © 2017
  An Improbable emergence – Book 3

- **Convergence of the Realms** © 2017
  An Improbable Emergence – Book 4

- **Escape from Inconsequence** © 2018

- **Reyes & Leeds** © 2018

- **Story of a Tale-Maker** © 2019

- **Nine Amber Pieces** © 2019

- **A Life Given, a Life Taken** © 2020